Lucky To Be Alive . . .

They were just outside of his rooming house and Longarm was about to open the building's door when he saw two men moving rapidly toward him along the sidewalk and then he saw both men draw pistols and raise them when they were only about twenty feet away.

Longarm shouted and reached across his belt buckle for the big Colt revolver resting on his left hip, butt forward. Both men opened fire. Longarm felt a bullet crease his shoulder and he heard Lucy cry out in pain. He snapped off two shots before he tore open the door and shoved Lucy headlong into the hallway. An instant later he felt another bullet strike him in the leg and he fell on the outside steps. Twisting around, he fired twice more and one of his attackers collapsed with a scream.

"You sonofabitch!" the wounded man cried, emptying his pistol.

Longarm rolled off the side of the front steps and shot the wounded man in the head.

The dying man's companion lost his nerve, whirled, and took off racing down the street. Longarm had one bullet left but he held his fire because there were innocent bystanders frozen with fear and indecision. He could not take the risk of accidentally killing one of them . . .

TABOR EVANS

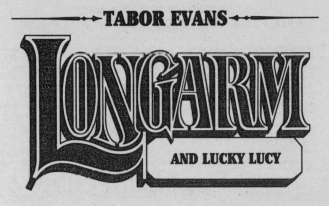

LONGARM

AND LUCKY LUCY

JOVE BOOKS, NEW YORK

THE BERKLEY PUBLISHING GROUP
Published by the Penguin Group
Penguin Group (USA) Inc.
375 Hudson Street, New York, New York 10014, USA
Penguin Group (Canada), 90 Eglinton Avenue East, Suite 700, Toronto, Ontario M4P 2Y3, Canada
(a division of Pearson Penguin Canada Inc.) • Penguin Books Ltd., 80 Strand, London WC2R 0RL,
England • Penguin Group Ireland, 25 St. Stephen's Green, Dublin 2, Ireland (a division of Penguin
Books Ltd.) • Penguin Group (Australia), 250 Camberwell Road, Camberwell, Victoria 3124, Australia
(a division of Pearson Australia Group Pty. Ltd.) • Penguin Books India Pvt. Ltd., 11 Community
Centre, Panchsheel Park, New Delhi—110 017, India • Penguin Group (NZ), 67 Apollo Drive,
Rosedale, Auckland 0632, New Zealand (a division of Pearson New Zealand Ltd.) • Penguin Books
(South Africa) (Pty.) Ltd., 24 Sturdee Avenue, Rosebank, Johannesburg 2196, South Africa

Penguin Books Ltd., Registered Offices: 80 Strand, London WC2R 0RL, England

This is a work of fiction. Names, characters, places, and incidents either are the product of the author's
imagination or are used fictitiously, and any resemblance to actual persons, living or dead, business
establishments, events, or locales is entirely coincidental.

LONGARM AND LUCKY LUCY

A Jove Book / published by arrangement with the author

PUBLISHING HISTORY
Jove edition / June 2012

Copyright © 2012 by Penguin Group (USA) Inc.
Cover illustration by Milo Sinovcic.

ISBN: 978-0-515-15093-3

JOVE®
Jove Books are published by The Berkley Publishing Group,
a division of Penguin Group (USA) Inc.,
375 Hudson Street, New York, New York 10014.
JOVE® is a registered trademark of Penguin Group (USA) Inc.
The "J" design is a trademark of Penguin Group (USA) Inc.

PRINTED IN THE UNITED STATES OF AMERICA

10 9 8 7 6 5 4 3 2 1

ALWAYS LEARNING   **PEARSON**

Chapter 1

Deputy United States Marshal Custis Long was enjoying a fine Saturday afternoon in downtown Denver while shopping for a new hat at Dexter's Mercantile. But he'd quickly lost interest in hats the moment a stunning young woman entered the cavernous store and went straight to the fabric department. Now the woman was at the cash register buying ribbon and lace while being waited upon by the store's owner, Mr. Alexander Dexter.

"I'm new in town," he overheard the tall, red-haired beauty tell the merchant, who seemed almost mesmerized by her lovely face and voluptuous figure. "And I was wondering if you could possibly give me some advice about downtown Denver's lodging accommodations. You see, I am currently staying at the Elkhorn Hotel. It is very pleasant and agreeable, but they do not offer long-term rates and I simply can't afford to stay there longer than necessary."

Mr. Alexander Dexter was in his mid-fifties and a

confirmed bachelor. Longarm had been shopping in the man's store for several years and judged him to be a serious-minded fellow who was a shrewd businessman but known to have a weakness for much younger ladies and high-stakes gambling. Longarm had heard rumors that both of those vices were about to send him into bankruptcy and ruin.

"Well," Mr. Dexter mused, taking his time and stroking his scraggly mustache as if he had been asked a question for the ages, "there are several places I might suggest."

"Then please do," the beauty urged, leaning forward just enough to display cleavage. "I am *not* a wealthy woman, but neither am I poor. I want some place that is safe, clean, and convenient."

"A ladies only establishment?"

"Well, I'm a widow, but I'd not mind a proper hotel with mannerly gentlemen."

"Good," Dexter said, smiling broadly. "I'm glad to hear that but terribly sorry about your late husband. He must have been quite young."

"His unexpected death was a great tragedy. We were very much in love and I lost him only last year."

"How very unfortunate!" Dexter exclaimed with an exaggerated show of sympathy. "Was he killed in an accident . . . or perhaps by a disease?"

"My dear husband was run over by a train."

Dexter blinked and Longarm stared as they both waited for a further explanation.

"A *train*?" Dexter finally blurted.

"Yes, my handsome Charles was wildly drunk and racing a train on one of his favorite horses when he foolishly tried to pass in front of the locomotive by jumping the rails. Unfortunately, his horse stumbled on the track and . . . well, it was a terrible mess. Charles was only twenty-five, and he was very well educated and the only son of the prosperous Horton family. Very well-respected people, and we had an almost fairy-tale courtship."

Alexander Dexter drummed his stubby fingers on the counter for a moment then said, "Forgive me for asking, but were you married very long?"

"Nineteen months. We didn't have any children, and I had little family of my own, all in Philadelphia. Charles, on the other hand, had a rather large and boisterous family. They all, sadly, drank like pagans . . . but they were fun and the men were exceedingly handsome and exciting."

"Charles had an uncle who was the secretary of state, but he was an awful little man and he kept trying to seduce me. Of course, I never told Charles because he would have been furious and there would have been a terrible fight. Charles would no doubt have killed his uncle as a matter of honor."

"Of course," Dexter said. "Then you are now alone, Mrs. . . .?"

"Mrs. Horton. Mrs. Lucy Horton."

Dexter took her hand and held it much too long. "It sounds as if you've had quite a life in a very few years, Mrs. Horton."

"Oh, I have! I've always been adventurous. Charles and I sailed around the world on a six-month-long honeymoon. We saw things that would take me hours and hours to even describe."

"I wouldn't mind listening to you for hours," Dexter said, finally realizing that the woman was trying to extract her hand from his clammy grip.

Lucy Horton sighed. "Charles was foolish to have tried to outrun and then cross in front of that train, and there are times when I feel anger at him rather than sadness."

"Perfectly understandable."

"You are very kind to be listening to my sad circumstances. And at least I have an older brother who has a Colorado ranch near a town called Cortez, which I understand is somewhere on the other side of the Rocky Mountains."

"Yes, it is," Dexter said, "but I'm sure that there is not much to be found in a place the size of Cortez. Nothing at all that would interest a worldly woman like yourself."

"Perhaps not, but Robert is all the family I have now so I'll go visit him in a few months. However, at the moment I need to find employment and rest up from my trials and travels. I'm from New Haven, and I do hope that the winters here in Colorado are not as severe as those back in Connecticut."

"Not at all!" Dexter exclaimed with assurance. "Oh, we do get *some* snow, but with our sunny winter days it rarely stays on the ground more than a few days and then it's all melted away."

Lucy brightened. "How nice to hear that."

Longarm couldn't help but grin because Dexter was really doing a whitewash about Denver's typically hard winters, which could be a real trial.

"Well, Mr. Dexter, thank you for your advice, and if you will tell me what I owe you for this lace and ribbon, I'll be on my way because I'm sure that this other gentleman is going to buy a new hat and that deserves your full attention."

"I'm in no hurry," Longarm replied, giving her his nicest and most disarming smile. "Take your time."

Dexter, who was about a foot shorter than Longarm, gave him a less than friendly smile and said, "This is Marshal Custis Long . . . better known by outlaws and criminals of the worst kind as Longarm."

Her appraisal was frank and unhurried. "What an unusual nickname, Marshal Long."

"Thank you."

Lucy paid her bill and turned to leave.

"Mrs. Horton," Dexter said, "I have a hotel that might be just perfect. It's reasonable and nearby."

"Is it respectable?"

"Oh yes!"

"Good," she told him at the door. "You see, I am fine with gentlemen as long as they're well behaved. I'll not stand for insults or advances."

Dexter could not completely hide his disappointment. Nevertheless, he cleared his throat and pursed his porcine little lips under a scraggly mustache and said, "I'd suggest the Porter House. I have roomed there for many years, and I can assure you that the hotel management is very selective about the kind of tenants they allow. I also happen to know that there is a second-floor vacancy . . . actually it's on the same floor where I live!"

Longarm could almost see the man salivate at the prospect of having the beautiful widow only a few paces from his own rooming house.

Lucy Horton smiled. "Could you please give me directions to the Porter House?"

"Of course!"

"Actually," Longarm interrupted, "I'm leaving now and I'll show you where it is. I'll be on my way, and my way just happens to go right past the Porter House. I'd be happy to escort you, Mrs. Horton."

"How kind of you, Marshal Long."

Dexter suddenly looked like he'd just bitten into a lemon.

Longarm opened the door for the woman, and he couldn't help but grin over his shoulder at the merchant. "I'll think about buying another hat some other time."

"Don't slam my door, Marshal."

"Wouldn't think of it," Longarm said, almost laughing as he closed the door much harder than was necessary and then offered his arm to Lucy. "Nice day for a stroll. Have you had time to see Cherry Creek and all the trees in blossom?"

"No, I haven't."

"Well, if you're not in a hurry and don't mind a slight detour, I'd be happy to show it to you now. There's a little walking path, and on a nice Saturday morning like this, there will be a lot of people out walking and families feeding the ducks."

"I really like ducks."

"So do I," Longarm said trying to sound sincere. "There's a little bakery about a block up the street. We can buy some bread to feed the ducks. They're always hungry."

"I know they are," she said happily. "Back in New Haven there are so many lakes, streams, and ponds. Canadian geese fly through both in the spring and the fall, and they are so noisy! You really can't satisfy their appetites, and if you tried . . . well, you'd go broke."

"The bakery sells day-old bread, and they know that a lot of it goes to the ducks."

"How kind of you, Marshal Long."

"Call me Custis."

"Then you can call me Lucy."

Longarm thought that was a great beginning. And as for the ducks, he'd never *really* bought day-old bread to feed them, but he knew some people did that, and he also knew that the idea would foster the impression that he was a bird lover . . . which he was not. Still, he didn't dislike ducks, and he had once thought about buying bread for them if he had nothing better to do and if it might catch the attention of a lovely and lonely young woman.

"How long have you been a marshal?" she asked as they strolled along Colfax Avenue.

"Oh, a good long while now."

"Do you like it?"

"Most of the time."

"Is it very dangerous?"

"It can be," he said as they waited to cross a street to the bakery he had in mind. "But I'm pretty careful, and I've done the job long enough that I know what to watch out for and expect from the worst types of criminals."

She looked up at him. "Have you . . ."

"Ever had to kill a man?" he said, anticipating her question because it was one that was frequently asked and he had learned to deal with it directly. "Yes, I have. Quite a few times, I'm afraid. But most of the men that I had to kill were out to kill me or had murdered others."

"Does that bother you?"

He shrugged his broad shoulders. "It does, depending on the man and the circumstances that led him to his downfall. You see, Lucy, sometimes a man is set on the wrong path from the moment of his birth. Usually it's his family, sometimes just circumstances."

"Like what exact circumstances are usually at fault?"

"Perhaps someone killed someone in a wanted man's family. Or he or his family were cheated, robbed, or badly wronged. There are often sad instances where drink, opium, or bad women have driven men to do things they would not normally do."

"But . . . but would you have to actually *kill* them if their backgrounds led them to such a sad fate?"

Longarm was hoping to change the subject, but Lucy seemed so sincere in her interest that he said, "When they try to kill me or someone else that is innocent, I really have no choice."

"I see," she said just before they crossed the street.

She didn't *really* see, he knew. But she was clearly a very intelligent as well as beautiful woman who was obviously moved by death and the everyday tragedies of life.

"Do you sleep well at night given the men who have died at your hand?"

"I . . . I sleep pretty well."

"You strike me as being a very brave man, Marshal. Brave but not as foolish as my late husband."

"I like to think that I'm not foolish," he replied. "A foolish lawman doesn't live to an old age. As for being brave, I never thought much about that. I just do my job and like to think that what I do is saving some innocent lives."

"I'm sure that it must be."

"Yes," he said, "I'm sure that it must be too."

"Are you married, Custis?"

"No."

"Ever been?"

He shook his head and smiled. "Nope."

"May I ask why not?"

"I'd like to tell you that it's just because I haven't met the right woman yet, but . . ."

"But that wouldn't be the truth."

"No, it wouldn't. The truth is that what I do is very

dangerous, and if I got married, had a family, well . . . well I might not come back from an assignment someday, and I'd leave a grieving and likely impoverished widow and some kids who'd never grow up knowing their real father."

"Yes," Lucy said, "I see. But you could change professions."

"And do what?" he asked. "Work behind the counter of some mercantile? Or a teller's cage at the bank? Or perhaps own a little shop and sit around all day trying to be nice to customers?"

"You make that all sound so . . . so distasteful."

"It would be to me. I'm a man that likes action, and I get bored doing the same thing day after day. I like to travel and meet people, and I try to be professional about my duty."

"You *are* wedded to your profession."

"I suppose that I am," he admitted. "Which all makes for very poor pickings for any woman with a husband on her mind."

"I don't want to get married again . . . at least not for many years. I loved Charles, but when you marry a man who comes from a very large and successful family, you discover that you are not taken very seriously."

Longarm looked closely at her. "It's hard to imagine than any man could fail to take you seriously."

"Because of my . . . my looks?"

"That and your mind."

She laughed. "You know no more about my mind than I know about yours, Custis."

"I know that you are a very interesting and thoughtful woman, which is somewhat rare, considering your beauty."

"Meaning that beautiful women are usually stupid?"

"I didn't say that."

"But you implied it."

Thankfully, they had reached the bakery. "Here we are. I'll buy a couple loaves of bread and we'll go feed some ducks."

"I'll enjoy that. Is the Porter House in sight?"

"Not yet," Longarm said, as they entered the bakery with its delicious aroma of freshly baked bread.

"Is it as nice and as respectable as Mr. Dexter promised?"

"I wouldn't know, because I couldn't afford to live there."

"But he said that it was *reasonably* priced."

"Yeah," Longarm said, "but reasonable for Alexander isn't reasonable for most of us. I'm afraid that the Porter House is very expensive."

"Hmmm," she mused as they began to look at the pastries.

Longarm, not wanting to seem miserly, had bought four loaves of day-old bread, and he knew that the ducks would still not be satisfied. But aside from the damned squawking ducks, the honest truth of the matter was that he had no intention whatsoever of later showing Lucy Horton the Porter House, where lecherous old Mr. Dexter would be anxiously lurking in the hallways tonight.

No, he instead would show her his *own* rooming house, and wasn't it just his luck that there happened to be an empty room adjoining his own.

Chapter 2

"If I lived in Denver," Lucy said, watching Cherry Creek flow past them and tossing the last of their stale bread to a horde of ravenous ducks, "this would probably be my favorite place to come on pleasant days."

Longarm nodded with agreement. "Coming here always gives me a sense of peace. Downtown is nice and there's always a lot going on, but it's good to be able to come here and just relax."

"And I take it your job doesn't allow you much time for relaxation."

"No," he said, "it doesn't. But there are boring stretches where I'll be stuck biding my time at the Federal Building waiting for an assignment. A day at the desk seems like a week to me."

"I imagine it would," she said. "Well, this has been very nice and I thank you, but I really should visit the Porter House and see if it might be a better place for me to stay for a while."

"I'll be happy to take you there," Longarm told her. "But like I said, it's pretty expensive."

"I'd still like to ask about their rates."

"Then you should definitely go in and speak to the hotel clerk," he said. "We can walk to the Porter House in less than twenty minutes."

Twenty-five minutes later, Lucy Horton exited the Porter House looking unhappy. Longarm was waiting for her out by the street. "How'd it go?"

"They want twenty-three dollars a week and I can't afford that much . . . or at least I don't want to pay that much. And the hotel desk clerk was . . . was much too forward and uppity. I guess that puts me back to square one at the Elkhorn Hotel."

"I have a much better idea."

She brightened considerably. "I'm listening."

"Lucy, I rent a very nice room just a block from where we fed the ducks on Cherry Creek. It's not as high-tone as this place, but it's clean, safe, and quiet."

Lucy's eyebrows lifted with suspicion. "Don't tell me that you're going to ask me to move in with *you*?"

"No," he said quickly. "I'm much too disorganized and messy for a lady like yourself . . . although that idea has crossed my mind about a dozen times in the last two hours."

"I'll just bet it has."

"But there is a vacancy next to my rooming house on the second floor."

"What a coincidence."

"Don't be so suspicious," he said. "The man who lived there moved out only last week. His empty room is furnished and the rate is good. Also, being as how you'd be rooming near a federal marshal, I can guarantee you that it would be safe."

"How much?"

"Ten dollars a week . . . maybe."

Lucy placed her hands on her hips. "What does 'maybe' mean?"

"I have a very persnickety landlady. Her name is Mrs. Emma Olsen and she's got a heart of gold, but she's nosy and strict concerning the rules she sets down for all her tenants."

"Have you lived there long?"

"Couple of years," Longarm replied. "Emma and I get along quite well. She knows that if I am in town and there is any trouble either inside the building or right outside, I'll handle it. She also is on an undying quest to find me a proper wife because she thinks my life is being wasted as a dedicated bachelor."

"I see. You are protective of Mrs. Olsen, and she is equally protective of you."

"That's about the size of it. Emma is tough, but fair. The place is quiet and I'm living on the second floor."

"I have to ask. Does Mrs. Olsen allow you to have *women* visitors?"

"Only those that are quiet and respectful," Longarm said, deciding to be entirely honest about it. "She doesn't like some of my lady visitors, but if they behave, she keeps her lips sealed tight. And there have been a few that she's actually liked enough to suggest that I marry."

They both laughed. "Well, since I have nothing to lose by visiting this woman and seeing if I pass her muster, let's go have a look."

"I think you'll be glad you did."

"As long as you understand that I'm not to be hectored or . . ."

Longarm threw up his hands. "I never press myself on the opposite sex. I promise you that I will always treat you as a lady and respect your wishes for privacy."

"Honest?"

"Honest," he said, sticking out his big paw. "You have my word of honor as a former Southern gentleman."

"From where?"

"West Virginia, Mrs. Horton." Longarm swept off his hat in a grand gesture and bowed slightly.

Lucy took his hand, and they shook on their understanding . . . one Longarm was sure would change in a few days . . . or perhaps weeks.

"Let's go," he said, "before Emma finds another tenant."

They were just outside of his rooming house, and Longarm was about to open the building's door when he saw two men moving rapidly toward him along the sidewalk. An alarm went off in his mind, and then he saw both men draw pistols from under their coats and raise them when they were only about twenty feet away.

Longarm shouted and reached across his belt buckle for the big Colt revolver resting on his left hip, butt forward. Both men opened fire. Longarm felt a bullet crease his shoulder, and he heard Lucy cry out in pain. His own gun cleared leather, and he snapped off two shots before he tore open the door and shoved Lucy headlong into the hallway. An instant later he felt another bullet strike him in the leg and he fell on the outside steps. Twisting around, he fired twice more, and one of his attackers collapsed with a scream while grabbing his stomach.

"You son of a bitch!" the wounded man cried, emptying his pistol.

Longarm rolled off the side of the front steps and shot the wounded man in the head. The dying man's companion lost his nerve, whirled, and took off racing down the street. Longarm had one bullet left, but he held his fire because there were innocent bystanders frozen with fear and indecision, and he could not take the risk of accidentally killing one of them.

Longarm knew he had been wounded twice, but he also knew that neither wound was serious enough to kill him if he received rapid medical attention to stop the serious loss of blood. Right now his main concern was Mrs. Lucy Horton. He crabbed over to the door and managed to struggle to his feet and fling it wide open.

"Custis!" Emma Olsen cried. "This woman is dying!"

Longarm knelt beside Lucy and saw blood flowing from a wound at her side. "Emma, grab me something to bandage this wound and then go find a doctor!"

Fortunately, the old landlady was steady and clearthinking. She dashed for her room, yelling, "I'll grab a towel and a sheet that you can tear apart for her!"

Longarm cradled Lucy in his arms. Her eyes were wide open and her face was twisted in a painful grimace. "Have I bought it?" she asked, tears rolling down her rosy cheeks. "Custis, tell me the truth. Am I going to die in this rooming house hallway?"

"No," he assured her. "You're shot, but I don't think it's fatal. Emma will be back in a moment and we'll get you bandaged up and . . ."

One of the other tenants, a bookkeeper man named Mark Greer, burst into the hallway. "What's going on!"

"Go find a doctor!" Longarm shouted. "There's one living just three doors down the street."

"I know exactly who you're talking about. Let's hope he's in today," Greer said, throwing open the door. "My god, there's a dead man lying at the bottom of our front stairs!"

"Mark, get the doctor!"

The door slammed, Emma hurried back with a towel and a sheet, and then she and Longarm set right to work stopping the blood flow.

"You just relax, dearie," Emma crooned over and over. "You're going to be all right, and a good doctor is on the way."

"What . . . what happened? Why did those two men suddenly. . . ." Lucy's words were cut off by a sharp gasp.

"They weren't trying to kill *you*," Longarm told the woman who was trying to stay conscious. "Lucy, you couldn't possibly have been their target."

"Don't be too sure of that," Lucy whispered as she closed her eyes and lost consciousness.

What seemed like an eternity later, Dr. Wilson burst into the hallway with Greer on his heels. Wilson was middle-aged and very expert at dealing with gunshot wounds. It took him only a few moments to cut Lucy's clothes away from her chest and examine the wound.

"Doc," Longarm asked, "is the bullet . . ."

"Let's roll her gently."

They turned Lucy, and the doctor clucked his tongue. "She's a very lucky woman. The bullet passed through her body just under the ribs. I'm almost certain it didn't penetrate any vital organs, and the other good news is that it exited just under the rib cage."

"Then she'll be all right?" Longarm asked.

"Once I clean the wound and bandage it properly, I think her prognosis is excellent. But I need to get her to a room close by. She's lost a great deal of blood and I don't want to risk having her moved all the way to my office."

"We'll take her to that vacant room next to yours," Emma said to Longarm. "I'll get some water boiling and she'll be comfortable there, Doctor."

"Good. Marshal, you appear to be losing a fair amount of blood yourself."

"I'll be fine."

"I'm the doctor and I'll be the one that decides that."

"Let's get Mrs. Horton up to that room first," he said. "Then when she's been fully taken care of, you can plug up my bullet holes."

"All right," Dr. Wilson agreed. "Let's move!"

An hour later, Lucy Horton was awake and lying in a soft bed. Longarm was sitting slumped in a chair with bandages on his shoulder and another around his leg. He was a mess but feeling damned good and grateful that they were going to recover.

"Custis," she whispered.

He pushed himself out of the chair and came to her side. "Hi, Lucy. The doctor says that you're going to make a full recovery. He says that you are a very lucky woman."

She managed a smile. "I've had more than my share of luck in life. Some people back in New Haven even called me Lucky Lucy. But right now I don't feel very lucky at all."

"I killed one of the assassins, and I'll get the other one no matter how long it takes."

"Did you recognize either man?"

"No," he said. "If I had to guess, I'd say they were probably family of someone I either shot to death or put in prison."

"They might have been trying to kill me," Lucy said. "You just might have it all wrong this time."

"And why would anyone try to kill a beautiful woman like you?" he asked.

"I'm not ready to tell you that just yet," Lucy replied. "And maybe they weren't actually trying to kill me . . . but I want you to know that it's a possibility."

Longarm shook his head in bewilderment. "I don't understand."

"Give it a little time," she offered as her fingers caressed his face, and then she drifted off to sleep.

Longarm returned to his chair. Emma was going to return soon, and then he'd hobble next door to his room, clean up, and change clothes. After that he'd come back to make sure that Lucy was doing well and try to sort out what had happened outside and why Lucy Horton thought that he might not actually have been the target of the two assassins.

There was a lot to think about and a hell of a lot to be thankful for today.

Chapter 3

"So," Marshal Billy Vail said, standing in Longarm's room and looking down on his wounded and favorite deputy marshal. "Why don't you start from the beginning when you met this woman and tell me everything that happened afterward?"

"Okay."

"And," Billy added, "what I really want you to tell me is who the dead man is and who was the son of a bitch that got away."

"I don't know either man," Longarm told his boss. "I'm quite sure that I've never met either one."

"Oh, come now! Think harder. Surely they must be a pair that has a grudge against you for putting them in prison."

Longarm shrugged. "Maybe they were just hired assassins."

"There is always that possibility," Billy admitted.

"Or," Longarm added, "they could be relatives or friends of someone I sent to the gallows."

"That too. I suppose."

"I got a good look at the one that I shot dead," Longarm said, "but not the one that got away."

"That's unfortunate," Billy mused. "It means that someone is in Denver that might try to kill you again."

"Don't you think that possibility has occurred to me?" Longarm asked. "But I'll tell you what really has me baffled."

"Keep talking."

"Mrs. Horton suggested that the two gunmen might actually be trying to kill *her*, rather than me."

"I haven't seen the woman yet, but I will soon. Tell me everything you know about her."

"I only met her today, at Dexter's Mercantile," Longarm began. "She's from New Haven, Connecticut, and has a brother named Robert Durham who is a rancher over near Cortez."

"And she is married?"

"Widowed," Longarm answered. "She was married into a well-to-do and prominent family from Philadelphia. Her husband's name was Charles Horton and he was killed in an accident."

Billy's eyebrows raised. "What *kind* of accident?"

"Charles Horton was drunk and racing a train. The train ran over and killed him and probably his poor racehorse."

Billy Vail's jaw dropped. "That's an incredible story."

"Yeah, isn't it though," Longarm agreed. "But from what I gather the husband was a wild man, and drunk more often than sober. Lucy said that all the men in the family were half-crazy and drank hard."

"So Charles Horton's widow, Mrs. Lucy Horton, shows up in Denver only a few days ago."

"That's right."

"For what reason?"

"Lucy led me to believe that she is broke and needs a temporary job to earn the money to go on to Cortez."

"Are you saying that the Horton family threw her out of Philadelphia after her drunken husband was run over racing a train?" Billy's expression was clearly one of disbelief.

"That's right."

"And you *believe* that wild story?"

"I do," Longarm confessed.

"Then you must also believe in the tooth fairy," Billy snorted.

"Boss, the woman was very nearly murdered."

"So how does the fact that the wealthy Boston family sent her packing without any money have anything to do with those two assassins?"

"Maybe it doesn't," Longarm admitted. "If I were placing a bet, I'd still say that those men were trying to kill me, not her. But what she said and the fact that I didn't recognize either gunman sure has raised some questions in my mind."

"I'll talk to her right now."

"Not today," Longarm said firmly. "Maybe not for a few days. She's lost a lot of blood and. . . ."

"*You've* lost a lot of blood!"

"She's in worse shape than I am," Longarm said stubbornly. "Let her rest a few days. Lucy sure as hell isn't going anywhere soon."

Billy didn't like this, but he had no choice but to agree. "I talked to the doctor, and he said that Mrs. Horton is a very lucky woman."

"Yeah. Lucy told me that she has always been lucky. That some of her eastern friends even called her 'Lucky Lucy.'"

Billy began to pace back and forth in the room, his mind clearly agitated. He stopped, turned to Longarm, and said, "And I'll just bet that she's pretty."

"She's *beautiful*," Longarm told the man. "Maybe not at this moment, but she's a real looker."

"Figures." Billy scoffed as he resumed pacing the floor. He pointed an accusing finger at his deputy marshal. "You *never* give much time to the ugly ones."

"Lucy Horton needed a place to rent more reasonable than the one she had, so I offered to help. It just so happens that the room right next door to mine recently became available."

"Yeah, sure," Billy quipped, voice filled with sarcasm. "How handy for you."

"Dammit, Billy, she's a lady and she's in trouble!" Longarm snapped with irritation. "What's wrong with me wanting to help her out in her time of need?"

"Nothing except I know you, Custis. You'll help her out all right. Help her in and out of your bed."

"Damn," Longarm swore, "you really are a jaded man. Haven't you ever heard of real *Southern* chivalry?"

"Of course I have, Custis, but I know you very well, and when you meet a beautiful woman that you want . . . Southern chivalry goes right out the bedroom window."

Longarm clucked his tongue as if he were severely disappointed in his boss's lack of faith in his simple act and intention of humanly kindness. But then again, Billy Vail did know him very well, and he was pretty near dead on the mark when it came to Longarm's lust for beautiful women.

* * *

The next few days passed slowly for Longarm. He spent a lot of time visiting with Lucy in her room, and he paid a workman to go get her belongings and transfer them over to his building. Lucy was traveling light. Just two valises and what she had been wearing that Saturday morning. It seemed strange to have so little if she had indeed been married to a wealthy man.

And because of that and other feelings, Longarm often tried to coax more background information from Lucy, but she had become quite closedmouthed about her past and the remark that she had made concerning the possibility that she had been the assassins' real target.

"I'm just very sorry that you were wounded," Lucy said one day with tears in her eyes. "You were really trying to help me, and look what happened."

"I'll survive."

"I know that," Lucy told him. "But you're losing time at work."

"The government is covering the time," he replied. "I'm not losing any pay, and I don't mind a little rest, and I enjoy the pleasure of your company."

"I'll never be able to repay you for all this kindness."

"I'm not so sure that's true."

Lucy smiled and cocked her head a little to one side. "You know something, Custis?"

"I know lots of things. What are you getting at?"

"I think that you are a real hound dog when you're on the fresh scent of a helpless young woman."

Longarm slapped his knee and guffawed. "Ha! I've never been called a 'hound dog' before, Lucy!"

"Come here," Lucy said, patting her mattress and smoothing her hair.

"I could be dangerous," he warned.

"So could I be."

"You're still pretty weak."

"And I'm a *lady*, Custis."

"You can be a lady and still be a woman in need of some loving."

"Be realistic. We're both weak from loss of blood."

"I'm not *that* weak," he answered as he sat down beside the woman and fingered a curl of her red hair. "I've never been *that* weak."

"I wonder." She reached a hand up and pulled him down beside her. "Could you and I really. . . . I mean physically . . ."

"Only one way to find out."

"I don't want to get hurt even worse than I have been," she whispered, lips brushing his lips.

"Are we talking physically or emotionally?"

"Maybe both."

"I won't hurt you either way," he promised, hand sliding under the bedcover and then along her bare thigh. "I'll be careful and it will make us both feel a whole lot better."

She hugged him tightly. "Are you sure?"

His finger slid into a damp, warm place, and she closed her eyes and moaned. "Custis, if you can do this without any physical damage, then I give you my full and complete consent to have your way with my body."

Longarm kissed her softly and then undressed. He saw the look in her eyes when she measured his largeness, and when he drew back the bedcovers and then gently unbuttoned her nightgown, he smiled.

"Even with that big bandage that Doc Wilson applied,

you're still about as beautiful a sight as a man could ever hope to see."

"I'm glad you think so. Just be very gentle."

Longarm eased his length down beside Lucy and cupped a large breast in his hand. His tongue darted out and Lucy sighed with pleasure. His finger went deeper into her hot treasure box and she began to squirm. Longarm eased her body onto her good side then lifted her leg and placed it on top of his hip.

"Open wide," he whispered, gently but firmly pushing into her luscious body. "Just lay still and let me do all the work."

"Gladly," she whispered, kissing him fiercely. "Have your way with this poor, wounded woman."

"That I intend to do," he vowed, thrusting deep into Lucy and then gripping her upraised thigh and rocking her a little back and forth.

Ten glorious, delicious minutes passed that way, him rocking her back and forth and thrusting while she groaned and shivered with pleasure. And when they finally came to the pinnacle of their pleasure, Lucy hooked her heel behind his butt and cried, "Now! Do it now!"

Longarm exploded, and if he lost a little of his control and hurt her slightly, he couldn't tell it, because Lucky Lucy was on fire with a raging, seemingly unquenchable desire.

Chapter 4

Longarm and Lucy were young and strong, and in the week that followed they made love often and stopped trying to keep up any pretense to their landlady that they weren't sleeping together.

Custis had suffered the less serious of the wounds, and so he often went downstairs to get groceries and meals. There was a little Chinese restaurant only a block away owned by a nice old couple, and their egg rolls, soups, and chicken were delicious beyond compare.

On Thursday afternoon as Longarm entered the rooming house, his landlady, Mrs. Emma Olsen, stopped him for a moment. "You are looking very chipper considering you were shot only five days ago."

"I'm feeling better every day, Mrs. Olsen."

"And what about the young lady?"

"The same. But she lost more blood and had a more serious wound than I did, so it might be another week before she feels strong enough to go up and down these stairs."

"Poor thing! When I saw her lying there in a pool of blood, I thought she was a goner. You really ought to be ashamed of yourself for putting that young woman's life in such jeopardy."

"Oh, I do!"

"Good. She's obviously sleeping with you. Given her wound and her fragile condition, you wouldn't be so beastly as to . . ."

"Of course not!" Longarm exclaimed, trying to look offended. "Good god, Mrs. Olsen, give me credit for having some morals and decency."

"I don't give you any credit at all after all the women I've seen you drag up my stairs," the old lady snapped. "But I know you never abuse them, and what goes on in that cave of yours is none of my business . . . or so I try to convince myself."

Longarm didn't have a reply for that and started to pass the woman.

"But, Custis, I want you to understand that I won't tolerate another scene like the one we had on Saturday. As you can easily imagine, it could scare my other tenants out of the building, and I won't have that. This is a nice, safe place, and having blood all over the front porch just won't do!"

Emma Olsen was upset, and Longarm knew she had quite a temper. So he said, "I'll try not to let anyone else attempt to kill me this close to the rooming house."

"Are you being smart-alecky?" she demanded.

"No, ma'am!"

"Well," the woman said, "I'm just not too sure that I like what is going on upstairs, and I'd better not hear any complaints from the other tenants. I like you, Custis, but I don't approve of your morals or way of life."

"I know that," he said, trying to look ashamed. "Maybe I should try to go to church once in a while."

His remark was made without sincerity, but Mrs. Olsen brightened. "Now that is the best thing I've heard from you in a good long while! And when she's well enough, you ought to invite that widow woman."

"I'll do that for certain."

"Good."

"Anything else, Mrs. Olsen?"

"Yes. Even though you are sharing the same bed, I expect rent on *both* rooms."

"Absolutely."

"And I won't allow this situation to go on forever. You're either going to have to move her back to her own room when she is strong enough to be on her own . . . or I'll ask her to leave."

"What if I married her?" Longarm asked out of idle curiosity.

"If you married her, you could save the second rent and I'd be very pleased about it."

"Glad to hear that."

"But you won't marry her, will you?"

"Even a goat can take a leap."

Emma's eyebrows rose in question. "And just exactly what does that mean?"

"I'm not sure," Longarm confessed. "But I thought it sounded clever."

"You're absolutely incorrigible and impossible, Marshal Custis Long. And I don't know why I didn't toss you out a long time ago."

"Maybe it's because you're a little sweet on me, Mrs. Olsen."

She reared back a fist, but he was already laughing and climbing the stairs.

Longarm was making love to Lucy again. This time she was on her hands and knees and he was behind. They had been in this position for more than ten minutes, just letting the pleasure build nice, slow, and easy.

"I can't believe that I'm doing this three and four times a day," Emma groaned. "I'm a seriously wounded woman recovering from a gunshot!"

"I know, and I'm giving you some medicinal injections."

Emma tossed her long red hair, reached between her thighs, and cupped his testicles. "You'd better be good to me or I'll crush these like grapes."

"I'm good, and you know that would be a tragedy for both of us," Longarm grunted.

Suddenly, there was a loud knock on their door.

"Oh, damn!" Lucy swore. "Don't make a sound and maybe whoever is out there will just give up and go away!"

But Longarm did make a sound. A rather loud, animal crying sound as he lost control and began to empty his seed. Lucy followed with her own cry of pleasure a moment later and then they collapsed on the bed, gasping for air.

More loud pounding.

"Go away!" Longarm shouted, rolling onto his back. "We're busy!"

"And I know what kind of busy you're busy at!" Billy Vail shouted. "Open this damned door! If you're strong enough to be so busy, you're strong enough to answer some of my questions."

"Shit," Lucy whispered. "That has to be your boss."

Longarm swore under his breath. "Give us five minutes, Billy. Go for a walk or something."

"Three minutes! I'm your boss, and I don't like to wait on people who are supposed to be working for me."

"Better get dressed fast," Longarm told Lucy. "I know Billy, and he isn't going to go away."

"This is pretty embarrassing, Custis."

"You'll live through it. Just . . . just pull the sheet up to your neck, and I'll throw on my pants and shirt. I'll try to get rid of him as fast as I can."

"But I'm leaking down below!"

Longarm pulled not only the sheet, but the bedspread over Lucy. She looked mad as hell, but when Billy began pounding on their door again, Longarm knew that there was no time to try and smooth Lucy's ruffled feathers.

"He'll think I'm the worst kind of harlot!"

"No," Longarm argued, "when Billy sees that beautiful face, all will be forgiven."

"Oh, shit," Lucy groaned, pulling the pillow over her head. "I don't want him to see me like this."

"Sorry."

Longarm quickly got dressed and opened his door. Billy looked plenty steamed and barged in past him to stare at Lucy, who was trying to comb back the damp locks from her face and put on a smile. It wasn't helping.

"So you're *Mrs.* Lucy Horton," Billy began.

"That's right. I'm a widow, in case Custis hasn't told you."

"He told me all right. And he also said that you suggested that he wasn't the real target when you were ambushed out in front of this building."

"I didn't say that," Lucy protested. "I merely told Custis

that he might not be the only one that had made an enemy in his lifetime."

Billy removed his hat and took a deep breath. "This is very embarrassing, talking to you like this."

"I agree," Lucy said. "So why don't you go away and come back later?"

"I'd like nothing better than to do that," Billy replied. "But the fact of the matter is that the local authorities are quite unhappy that there was a shoot-out out front last Saturday and that a man died while two people were wounded. They want some answers, and it's only because my federal office has done them some important favors that I've been able to forestall them from coming here days ago."

"Thank you for that," Lucy said. "What can I tell you that I haven't already told Custis?"

"Custis hasn't been back to the office and he hasn't told me much of anything except that you were married to a maniac who died racing a train and that he and his entire family are wealthy people who live in Philadelphia and the men of the family all drink to extreme."

"That's about the size of it," Lucy said, relaxing and drawing the covers up tighter around her chin. "And the fact that the men are very handsome and powerful."

"What I find most curious," Billy said, drawing up a chair without invitation, "is that you came to Denver without any money."

"I would imagine a lot of people arrive in this town broke or nearly so."

"Don't try and be cute with me, Mrs. Horton. If your deceased husband's family was wealthy, then why in the world wouldn't you have inherited or been given some of that wealth?"

"I didn't like them," she said flatly. "At least I didn't

like the men of the family. They were all . . . excuse my French . . . completely self-absorbed assholes."

Billy's jaw dropped. "But yet you married one?"

"I didn't know he was a complete asshole when he courted me," Lucy said. "And Charles did manage to keep his father and brothers pretty much at bay. I was shielded from the truth about the Horton family, and after we were married it was too late for me."

"So your husband's death was a relief?"

"A release," she corrected. "I would have left him eventually. I refused to sleep with him after the first month, and I would never have borne him a child."

Billy expelled a deep breath. "I'll say this for you, Mrs. Horton, you strike me as being very forthright and honest."

"Glad to hear that, Marshal Vail. Did you have any other 'curiosities' that I might be able to satisfy?"

"Of course I do! If those two men were not attempting to kill my finest deputy and were really after you . . . then why?"

"I have no idea." Lucy pulled her arms out from under the covers and threw them up in the air. "It's a complete mystery, and there is that chance that I was not the target."

Billy ran his fingers around his hat's brim. "Mrs. Horton, the local authorities are going to insist on speaking to you, and they're not going to be as forgiving or understanding as I'd like to be."

"I'll tell them exactly what I've told both you and Custis. Nothing less and nothing more, because there isn't any more to say."

"Now, I'm afraid that I doubt you are telling me the truth."

Lucy actually smiled. "Marshal Vail, I think we have exhausted this line of discussion. And I really am exhausted. Would you please excuse me and go away?"

Billy flushed with anger and popped out of his chair. "I'll leave you fully understanding why you are. . . . exhausted. Custis can be a load, I'd imagine."

It was Longarm's turn to blush with anger. "Billy, you're stepping over the line with that remark."

"Sorry." He went to the door, turned, and said, "Custis, given what I've just seen, I'm sure that you are physically capable of coming to my office first thing tomorrow morning, where we will have a nice, long talk."

"Yes, sir."

"Good day, Mrs. Horton. I'm glad to see that you are enjoying your recovery with so much vigor."

Lucy's mouth opened, but Longarm shot her a glance that said she should swallow her outrage and let the remark pass.

Billy left the room, and Longarm took a chair.

"I don't think I like your boss very much," Lucy told him. "In fact, I don't think that I like him at all."

"He's a very good man," Longarm said defensively. "But like he said, he's under some pressure from the locals, and he wants to find out what really happened so that it doesn't happen again."

"I'm all for that too."

"Then maybe," Longarm suggested, "you should tell me what you haven't told me so far."

"There is nothing to tell," Lucy insisted. "And if you aren't satisfied with that answer, I believe I'll get out of this bed and go next door to my own bed!"

Longarm shook his head. "Stay put," he said. "Simmer

down and let's talk about what we're going to have for supper."

"I'd find that conversation acceptable, Custis." Lucy smiled and then tried to hide a giggle.

"What's so funny?"

"The look on that man's face when he came in here and saw me with the covers pulled up to my chin. I can't even imagine what he was thinking and how he managed to remain composed."

Longarm had to chuckle some himself. "Billy has seen about everything in his time. He wasn't always the head of our entire department and a desk man. When he was younger, he was out in the field risking his life and hunting down outlaws just like I do right now."

"And can you see yourself in his position in ten or fifteen years?"

"You mean shuffling papers and writing reports to Washington, D.C.?"

"If that's what he does, yes."

"No, I can't see myself doing that."

"Well then, you need to think of a new line of work."

"Yeah, you suggested that a time or two already."

"I might have an idea or two."

"Let's hear them."

"I'm not ready to talk about that for a while."

"Just like you're not ready to tell me why those two men might have been out to take your life?"

Lucy dropped the covers and exposed her lovely breasts. "We were having such a nice afternoon. Must we argue now?"

Longarm couldn't help but swallow hard. "No," he said, starting to unbutton his pants. "I don't see why we have to do that at all."

"Me neither," she said, cocking a finger in his direction as she swept off the bedcover and sheets. "Let's take up where we left off."

"But I seem to remember that we had finished."

Lucy grinned. "New beginnings are the thing, Custis. New beginnings."

Longarm wasn't about to argue that fact, not while Lucy was spreading her legs and looking like a love goddess.

Chapter 5

Longarm was not happy about going to see the local authorities. Generally speaking, the local lawmen were very possessive of their jurisdiction and quite jealous of the fact that they were paid less than the federal lawmen. Cooperation, at its best, was pretty much a day-to-day thing, although Billy Vail had worked hard to keep the local sheriff involved in whatever his federal office had going on in Denver. Still, Longarm knew that, given the clashes of egos and authority between the locals and the federal people, the relationship was hardly more than a grudging truce. It was that way in Denver, and it was that way when Longarm traveled on his assignments to towns both big and small.

"Just another half a block and we'll be there," Longarm said, supporting Lucy as they walked slowly down the sidewalk along Cherokee, passing stores and other pedestrians.

"I really have nothing to say to these people that I

haven't already told you and your boss," Lucy said, clearly upset. "And I don't understand why I have to do this!"

"Just help my office out a little today," Longarm pleaded. "I'll do most of the talking and they might want us to sign a statement. It's all politics and bureaucracy, something that needs to be done in order to keep the peace."

"All right," she agreed. "But I won't be prodded or insulted."

"And I won't allow that to happen," Longarm promised. "Sheriff Clyde Goddard is an honest and decent man, and I know that he'll be respectful. But he's ambitious, and I'm sure that he's got his eye on becoming Denver's next mayor. What Goddard wants is to make sure that it's his office that catches the man that wounded us and that he gets the credit for the capture."

"Has he found out any more about the man that you killed in front of the rooming house?"

"Not to my knowledge." Longarm opened the door to the local sheriff's office. "Just relax, Lucy. We won't be here all that long."

"I hope not, because I really don't feel well."

"You felt pretty well last night," he said, trying to coax a grin out of the redheaded woman.

"Well," she said, managing a smile, "I was feeling pretty good. That was excellent wine that you brought up to go with our dinner. Two bottles and my head is still a little heavy this morning."

"It'll feel better soon," he said, escorting her through the front of the office and shaking hands with a short, heavyset deputy. "We're here to see the sheriff. He's expecting us."

The deputy gave Lucy a good quick and hungry look up and down and said, "Right this way."

They were ushered into Goddard's office, which was actually nicer than the one Billy had in the Federal Building. Goddard was easily six-foot-five-inches tall, skinny and bald. His face was craggy and his eyes were set far back in his skull. He looked like a man who had a constant case of indigestion, but Longarm knew him to be a rather humorous man when he let down his guard, and he had a fine family that he liked to brag about given the slightest excuse.

"Mrs. Horton," Sheriff Goddard said, extending his huge hand. "I am so sorry to have had you come here when you are not fully recovered. But we do need to have this meeting, and I have a little paperwork that I need for both you and Marshal Long to look over and sign."

"What kind of paperwork?" Lucy asked suspiciously.

"Well," Goddard replied, motioning them both to take seats, "I took the liberty of talking to Marshal Vail and from that meeting had an account of the shooting typed up for your signature. Of course, if there are details that I have misunderstood, then we'll have the papers reworded, retyped, and sent over to your room."

"I see."

"But mainly, I just wanted to hear an account of the shooting straight from your lips."

"*Her* lips, but not mine?" Longarm questioned.

"Both," Goddard said smoothly. "But I'd like to hear what Mrs. Horton has to say first."

Lucy gave Longarm a sideways glance, and when he nodded, she began, "We were walking toward the rooming house where Marshal Long lives and suddenly these two men opened fire on us."

"Whoa," Goddard said, "not so fast. Where had you been before the attack?"

"Out by Cherry Creek."

"Doing exactly what?"

"Feeding ducks day-old bread."

It wasn't the answer Goddard was hoping for, and he looked exasperated but recovered fast. "Go on, Mrs. Horton."

"Well, as I was trying to say, these two men opened fire on us without provocation or any warning. Custis killed one, but not before we were both wounded. I blacked out, but I heard that Custis shoved me through the rooming house door and killed one of the attackers, but the other got away."

"Please consider this next question very, very carefully. Did you recognize either man?"

"No," Lucy replied. "And I've told that to both Custis and his superior officer, Marshal Vail."

Goddard steepled his long, bony fingers together under his pointy chin. "And why do you think that these men attacked you and the marshal?"

"I have no earthly idea."

"And yet," Goddard said, "I understand that you told Custis that the attackers might actually be trying to kill *you* . . . not him."

"I did say that."

"Why?"

Lucy shrugged. "My deceased husband's family is very powerful and vindictive. They might have hired those men to follow me to Denver."

Goddard frowned, glanced at Longarm, then back to Lucy. "Just out of . . . what? Spite?"

"They are not nice men."

"Hmmm," Goddard mused. "If they wanted you dead out of spite, why wait until you came all the way to Denver?"

Lucy stared at her hands now folded in her lap. "I left Philadelphia after having a fight with my dead husband's father and one of his brothers."

"May I ask the cause of this 'fight'?"

"You may ask, but I'm not going to tell you," Lucy said firmly. "It was personal and family business and none of yours."

Goddard turned to Longarm. "Were you aware of this?"

"No," Longarm admitted. "But I suspected it."

"And don't you think that perhaps it *is* our business to learn the circumstances behind this fight between Mrs. Horton and her family?"

"They are *not* my family!" Lucy spat. "My family lives in New Haven, Connecticut. They are good, honest, and hardworking people. The Horton family is wicked, unscrupulous, and ruthless."

"And your husband was all of that?" Goddard asked.

"My ex-husband was all of that, only I didn't realize it until a good while after we were married."

Sheriff Goddard drummed his fingertips on his big desk. "Mrs. Horton, if you don't reveal your past then how can either Custis or myself hope to spare you from another attack in the future?"

"I doubt that there will ever be another attack, and neither Custis nor myself is certain that I was the target. For all we know the attackers were trying to kill him and not myself."

"Yes, I understand that," Goddard said, not sounding very convinced of the possibility. "The dead man has of course been buried, so you can't look at him and possibly make identification."

"I couldn't have identified the shooter even a moment after he hit the sidewalk," Lucy snapped. "I told you that neither of us recognized either assassin."

"Hmmm, well, it seems that we have come to the blind end of an alley this morning. You don't seem to have anything to tell me that will help catch the one that got away."

"I'm sorry, but I don't."

"Custis?" the sheriff asked, eyes shifting. "Can you add anything?"

"No," he said. "I wish that I could, but I can't. It happened very fast. I think that Mrs. Horton and I are both fortunate even to be alive."

"It would seem so." Goddard sighed. "And who do *you* think was the real target . . . yourself or Mrs. Horton?"

"I've asked myself that a hundred or more times since the shooting, and I can't say either way, Sheriff."

Goddard shrugged his narrow shoulders, leaned forward, and said, "This is getting us nowhere. I had hoped that one or the other of you would have something to add to this case that would help us catch and prosecute the gunman that got away."

"I'm sure either your office or mine will find the man that escaped."

"I damn sure hope so. I understand that you, Mrs. Horton, are living in the same rooming house as Marshal Long."

"Yes, but . . ."

"In case we need to get in touch in a hurry, what is your room number?"

"Seven."

"And your room number, Marshal?"

"Eight. Rooming house number eight."

Goddard looked from one to the other of them. "How convenient!" A pause. "For *us* that is . . . if we need to talk to you in a hurry."

"Yes, it would be," Longarm said in a clipped tone, his face turning hot with suppressed anger.

Sheriff Clyde Goddard was really playing the part of an aggrieved party to this mystery, and he wasn't being very gracious with Lucy. In fact, Longarm was certain that this room number thing was a ruse to embarrass them both. "Sheriff, I understand that you have a statement that we need to sign before we go."

"That's right. Just for the record."

"Of course," Longarm replied. "Always good to have the record on paper."

"That's right. And if there is another attack and either of you is killed, I want what we have so far written down in black and white."

"Always wise to cover your rear, Sheriff. Never know when something can come up behind and bite you on the ass."

Goddard's eyes narrowed, and it was clear he did not appreciate Longarm's remark. "I'll get the statement and you can sign it and leave. But if you remember something that will help us get to the bottom of this attack, then I fully expect that you will come back here and tell me about it without any reserve or hesitation."

"That's a promise, Sheriff."

"Fair enough then. I can't say that I'm happy about this meeting, but I'll just have to trust that you are both being forthright and honest."

"Understood."

The sheriff unfolded from his chair and left them with his door open.

"He doesn't believe me," Lucy whispered.

"Why didn't you tell me that you and the family had a

big blowup?" Longarm asked, not happy to learn this fact in Goddard's office.

"I was sure you suspected it, and it seemed of no consequence."

"It is of some consequence in that it makes the odds that those men were after you rather than me a whole helluva lot higher."

"Don't be upset with me," Lucy said, taking his hand. "I really am not up to bearing that right now."

Longarm felt a rush of guilt. "I'm sorry," he apologized. "We can talk about this fight you had with your late husband's family later."

"I'm not going to talk about it later," she said, chin lifting. "What happened is too personal."

"And we haven't been 'too personal' in my room since we were both wounded?"

"Of course we have!" Lucy's eyes misted. "I really can't talk about this, and you should let it be."

Longarm was about to answer when Sheriff Goddard plodded in and dropped some papers on his desk. "Both of you can read the statement, and if you basically agree that the facts are correct, please sign it at the bottom of the last page."

Lucy said, "You read it, Custis. If it is all right with you, then I'll sign after you."

Longarm read the statement, found it to be factual and correct, and signed it. Lucy followed, and ten minutes later they were back on Cherokee and headed toward their rooming house.

"How are you feeling?"

"A little weak and dizzy," she admitted. "But I'll be all right once we get back to the rooming house."

Longarm was about to say something, but all thought

of it vanished when a bullet whip-cracked past him and Lucy. He pushed her down hard behind a horse watering trough, eyes swinging around in a full circle and seeing pedestrians scatter as his Colt came into his hand. Something inside told him to look up and across the street to the second-story rooftop of a brick building.

A rifleman was taking aim for a second shot, and Longarm snapped a bullet in his direction, knowing it was wild and errant.

The rifleman vanished.

"Oh my god!" Lucy wailed. "Is it the same man?"

"I'm sure it is. Stay down. I'm going after him."

Before Lucy could argue or even speak, Longarm jumped up and ran across the street and into the building where the rifleman had taken a firing position upstairs.

"Hey!" a fat man in a cook's apron cried in confusion. "What . . ."

"Where are the stairs to the rooftop!"

"Who . . ."

Longarm reached inside his vest, flashed his federal officer's star, and the cook pointed to the rear of the café. "Back there, Marshal!"

He found the door to the stairwell, threw it open, and with his leg wound throbbing as he began to limp, Longarm struggled up the narrow and creaking wooden stairs to the rooftop. He threw open the door and jumped sideways, expecting a bullet. None came. The rooftop was empty. The rifleman was gone.

Longarm charged across the roof to the edge that gave him a clear view to Cherokee. He saw Lucy crouched behind the water trough, and when she saw him, she shouted something that he could not understand. Shaking his head, he cupped a hand behind his ear, and she pointed toward the gap that separated his building from the next. Longarm ran over to that side of the roof, peered down, and just caught a glimpse of a man jumping off the fire escape ladder and sprinting out of sight.

"Damn!" he shouted in anger and frustration. "That son of a bitch has more lives than an alley cat!"

Five minutes later he was back with Lucy. She was badly shaken but otherwise unharmed.

"Your wound?" he asked, touching her dress. "It didn't tear open when I shoved you to the sidewalk?"

"No," she said, "but I see a stain down on your leg where you were shot. Custis, you're losing blood!"

He clamped a hand on his pants leg and winced with pain. "I'll be fine. Probably just tore the scab on the stair's rail when I was trying to get onto the roof. I remember bumping into it hard."

"We need to get you over to Dr. Wilson right now."

"Good idea."

This time it was Lucy who helped the hobbling United States marshal down the street to the doctor's office. Fortunately, the doctor was in, and when he examined the reopened wound, he said, "You set yourself back a week, Marshal. What the hell happened this time?"

"About the same thing that happened last time."

"You mean . . . you mean you were shot at again?"

"That's right. I'm almost sure it was the same attacker, but this time he had a rifle and a rooftop vantage point. Son of a bitch is a lousy shot for certain or I'd be dead."

"You . . . or the woman?"

Longarm glanced across the examining room at Lucy. "We haven't yet figured that one out, Doc. But we will before long."

Dr. Wilson looked at one of them and then the other. He understood what the marshal was saying between the lines. But that was their business and none of his own, so he rebandaged the leg in silence and when he was finished said, "Try to take it easy and not get shot at again, Marshal Long. The human body has only so much blood to lose . . . then it dies."

"I understand and I'll do my best."

"I'm sure that you will," the doctor said, glancing at Lucy. "I'm sure you *both* understand."

Longarm waited until they were alone, and then he leaned toward Lucy and said, "Like it or not, we're going to talk about Philadelphia."

"I can't."

"You *have* to!"

Lucy sobbed and began to cry, but Longarm stood firm. Someone had tried to kill them . . . twice. He had to know what the hell was going on, and that meant he had to learn more about Lucy Horton and her mysterious past.

"Lucy, I'm sorry, but when we get back to my rooming house, we'll have a shot or two of whiskey and then it's tell-the-truth time."

But she emphatically shook her head.

"You won't tell me even after what happened?"

"I can't and I won't," she whispered.

"Lucy, our lives depend on finding out who is after us."

"They're after *me*."

"But . . ." He saw the doctor standing in the next room, obviously listening.

"We can talk back at my room."

"I'm not going back to your room."

"Then . . ."

"Loan me the stagecoach fare to Cortez," she begged,

voice both fierce and desperate as she wiped her eyes with a handkerchief. "I'm leaving Denver on the next stage."

"But . . . but why?"

"Will you loan me the money, Custis? I promise on my word of honor that I will repay you ten times over. But I have to have that money and get out of this town!"

He could see that she was very near to her breaking point. To do anything but say yes might push Lucy Horton right over the brink. "All right," he finally agreed. "I'll loan you the money, and even take you to the stagecoach office. There's a coach that leaves every day, and it departs Denver in about two hours."

She threw her arms around his neck, tears wet on his cheek. "Thank you, Custis!"

He held her tight, so confused, hurt, and desolated that he had no words left to say.

Chapter 6

Longarm went to his bank and drew out seventy-five dollars, which was a fair chunk of his meager savings. When he and Lucy exited the bank, he handed her the cash. "I'll walk you over to the rooming house and help you pack your things, then we'll go to the stage line."

Lucy couldn't hide the anxiety in her voice. "Do you think that they might already be booked for today's run?"

"Not likely," Longarm said. "But we don't have time to go there first to check."

"All right."

They made short work of their visit to the rooming house. Lucy had only a few possessions, which still seemed remarkable given her former wealth.

"I'll take that little valise," she said, pulling it from his grasp.

"It's a nice one. Beautiful leather. Buckles look to be made of pure silver."

"It's made of ostrich skin."

"A bag made from the skin of a *bird*?"

"That's right. A very large Australian bird."

"If it's a bird's skin, no wonder it's so soft." He looked around. "Anything else?"

"If I left anything, you can hold it for me," she told Longarm.

He really was going to miss Lucy, and this was a note of hope. "Does that mean you intend to come back to Denver?"

"I . . . I don't know. But maybe."

She started to leave her room, but Longarm gently grabbed her wrist. "I'm not sure if this is such a good idea, Lucy."

"As long as we're together, your life is very much in danger, Custis. The sooner I go the safer you'll be."

"I'm not afraid of danger."

"I know that," she told him. "But I don't want you hurt any more than you already have been."

Longarm released his grip. "I just wish you'd tell me who is after you and why."

"It's better that I don't," she said, kissing him on the lips. "Let's go before I miss that stagecoach."

"Yeah, we can't let that happen."

"I'll miss you too, Custis. More than you can imagine."

"Sounds nice."

"Don't make this any harder on us than it already is."

"I could take some time off and come visit you in Cortez."

Lucy smiled. "I'm not sure if my brother and I will get along all that well or if I'll stay in Cortez. Let's just let it play out and see what happens."

"Sure."

Ten minutes later they were at the stagecoach office buying Lucy a one-way ticket to Cortez, Colorado. It cost $28.75. "I should give you back some money," Lucy told him as she reached for her purse.

"Naw, keep it because you may need it on the other side of these mountains."

"I'll keep my promise and repay you ten times over," she said as the driver climbed up into the driver's box and the other passengers began to take their seats.

"Don't worry about it," Longarm said sincerely. "Just write me a letter when you get settled, so that I know you made it to your brother's ranch and that everything is fine."

"I'll do that. I'll write as soon as I arrive."

Longarm helped Lucy up into the coach, which had five other passengers. There were two young cowboys on the stagecoach, so he called, "Take care, *Mrs.* Horton!"

"I'll do that," she promised as the stagecoach lurched forward and headed down the road.

Longarm waved good-bye . . . but Lucy didn't.

After seeing Lucy off for Cortez, Longarm didn't want to go back to his empty room, so he walked over to his office and filed a report of the second ambush. Billy Vail called him into his office.

"So you were shot at again?"

"That's right."

"And the rifleman got away clean."

"He did."

Billy looked very unhappy. "I couldn't help but notice the fresh bloodstain on the leg of your trousers."

"I banged it on the stairs trying to get up on top of a building in a hurry. Dr. Wilson said that it wouldn't be a problem."

"The problem is that we have an ambusher in Denver who's twice tried to put out your lights."

Longarm leaned forward in his chair. His mind was still awhirl over Lucy's sudden departure and the mystery that she concealed. "I'm pretty damned sure that the ambusher was trying to kill Mrs. Horton . . . not myself."

"Why do you think that?"

"The bullet seemed meant for her. I know it's impossible to say for certain, but the slug passed her head much closer than mine. And there is something else."

"Keep talking, Deputy."

"Before she left, Lucy said that I'd be safer without her."

Billy rocked back in his swivel chair and shook his head. "So, Mrs. Horton is running from someone who very much wants her dead."

"It appears so."

"And do you think he might have followed you to the stage line and seen you put her on board the coach bound for Cortez?"

"I don't think so," Longarm answered after a long pause. "I was watching our backs all the way from my rooming house to the stage line, and I couldn't detect anyone following."

"Hmmm . . . I wonder."

Longarm stood with a worried frown on his handsome face. "Dammit, Billy, I should have gone with her to Cortez."

"And what good would that have done?"

"If the rifleman is the same man that attacked us at the rooming house, he'll not give up until he's killed her. He'll figure out that she's gone to Cortez and follow. Without me at her side, I doubt Lucy will stand much chance."

"Sit down," Billy said gently. "There's a lot here to

consider. First off and despite what she said today, you can't be certain that someone isn't really trying to kill you . . . not her. And second off, Mrs. Horton might not even be going to Cortez."

Longarm blinked. "But . . ."

"I don't think she has been entirely honest with you, Custis. She's hiding things about her past, and I believe that her beauty has blinded you to the fact that she is . . . well, *devious*."

Longarm didn't like the sound of that opinion, but he had to admit there was some truth to what his boss was saying.

"If she didn't go to Cortez, where would she go?"

"We may never find out," Billy said. "She might get off anywhere between here and Cortez and find other places to hide or even strike out for somewhere entirely different."

"She doesn't have much money. Only about forty or fifty dollars after the fare to Cortez."

"Maybe she has a lot more money than you know."

"I doubt it."

Billy shrugged. "I think that your . . . affection for the widow Horton has clouded your reasoning."

"Lucy promised she'd write the moment that she arrived in Cortez."

"Day after tomorrow?"

"Yep."

"If she keeps her word, you should get her letter in five or six days. A week at the longest."

"I'd say so."

Billy smiled. "Why don't you just try and sit tight and recover from your wounds until then?"

"You know I'm not one to sit around."

"I know. But you can come to the office each day, and I won't have to dock you any pay for being out. In a week . . . ten days on the outside . . . if you haven't heard from her yet, then . . ."

"Then whoever is after Lucy might have found her and she might already be dead."

"Give it ten days, Custis. If you haven't heard from Mrs. Horton in ten days, then you have my support to take a stagecoach to Cortez and find out what happened to her . . . if anything."

"It's going to be a long ten days."

"I know that. But the woman didn't ask you to go with her to Cortez, and she strikes me as being smart as well as clever and beautiful. And I'll tell you something else that has crossed my mind and obviously hasn't crossed yours."

Longarm plopped down in a chair. "Shoot."

"We don't know if Lucy Horton is her real name. We don't know if she has a brother who ranches outside of Cortez named Robert Durham. We don't know if she was raised in Connecticut or was married into wealth in Philadelphia. In short, she may be someone with an entirely different name and history."

"I just don't think she'd lie to me about everything," Longarm said stubbornly.

"If she lied about one thing, she's quite capable of lying about *everything* in her past."

Longarm was getting mad. He came to his feet and headed for the door. "I'll get a letter from her and probably the money I loaned her for the ticket in ten days or less."

"I hope so."

"I will, Billy! The woman may not have been entirely candid and honest with me, but she's a good person who is being hunted by at least one killer. And she's a person of her word . . . too."

"In ten days we'll know," Billy told him. "And in the meantime I'll be sending out a few telegrams. One to the marshal of New Haven, Connecticut, asking if he knew Mrs. Horton or knows the Durhams, her family. The second to Philadelphia."

Longarm whirled around and limped back to confront Billy. "Send one to New Haven . . . fine! But if you send one to Philadelphia, there is a good chance that the authorities there will contact the Horton family. If they do that, then if the family doesn't already know, they'll learn for sure that Lucy was here, and then they might be able to track her to Cortez. That just can't happen!"

Billy threw up his hands. "All right. I won't send any telegrams to Philadelphia . . . yet."

Longarm relaxed. "Thanks."

"Did you go and report this latest shooting to Sheriff Goddard?"

"The hell with him."

"I'll send a man over to tell him what happened. He may want you to come back to his office and make another report."

"And I may decide that I won't do it," Longarm said angrily.

"Custis, don't do that. If you and I are friends . . . and we most certainly are . . . don't get Goddard and myself into a contest of wills. I don't need that kind of grief."

"All right, Billy. For the sake of our friendship, I'll go along with the sheriff. But he wasn't very kind to Lucy and I'm not about to do him any extra favors."

"Fair enough."

Longarm went out into the main office and took a seat

at his desk. A desk that he hated and spent as little time behind as possible. There was a stack of papers that he needed to read, some to respond to as well. Bureaucracy—you just never got away from it unless you were out somewhere doing the real work of being a United States deputy marshal tracking down killers and criminals.

Chapter 7

Longarm waited ten days and drank a bit more than he should have. But each day he also forced himself to exercise, and that included long, brisk walks. He had two heavy rocks that he'd collected from along Cherry Creek, and he used them to build his arm and chest strength. Sometimes, thinking of Lucy Horton, he drove himself past his normal limits.

He visited Dr. Wilson's office twice to have his bandages changed, and the physician pronounced him fully recovered. "You've got a few more scars to add to your impressive collection, but you're fit to go out in the field whenever you're ready."

"I'm always ready to be on the move," Longarm replied.

"Have you heard from that beautiful young woman yet?"

"No."

Dr. Wilson frowned. "I wasn't too happy to learn that

she'd taken a stagecoach all the way over the Rockies to Cortez. Those stages can be rough riding and . . . well, I wish she'd have waited until now."

"She was determined to go see her brother and to get out of danger."

"Understandable," Dr. Wilson said, "but who's to say that danger isn't waiting in Cortez?"

"Not me," Longarm told the doctor. "Fact is, I'm wondering if she's still alive or not. Or even if she has a brother named Robert over there."

"Only one way to find out, and a man should settle his mind or his body doesn't heal properly."

"So are you prescribing that I go to Cortez for my health?"

"That's right. A physician doesn't always heal with pills or elixirs or cathartics. Sometimes a good physician has to address the state of his patient's mind and make a strong recommendation."

"What makes you think that my mind is troubled?"

"Well, for one thing you aren't eating enough and you've lost about twenty pounds since you were first wounded. For another, there are some pretty dark rings under your eyes telling me you're not sleeping very well. And finally, your eyes are a bit bloodshot, and I suspect you've been drinking too much lately."

"You should have been a detective, Doc."

"I *am* a detective. A medical detective. And you need to go to Cortez."

"I will," Longarm said, making up his mind. "I'm going to leave tomorrow."

"Why wait a day?"

"Because the stagecoach has already left Denver."

"Good reason. Just try to relax and put on some weight while you're gone, and to sleep better."

"I'll do my best," Longarm promised as he paid the man and left to go buy his ticket to Cortez.

The stagecoach ride over the Rocky Mountains was long and difficult. They hit three storms crossing the huge range, and the worst was while trying to get through a pass that was nearly twelve thousand feet high. Up at the timberline the air was cold and the snow was still hugging the highest peaks and a hard wind seemed to constantly blow from the northwest.

The three other passengers traveling with Longarm were an older couple that never stopped complaining about their health, the potholed roads, the driver's swearing, the dust, the wind, the rain, the cold, and even the scenery, which was pretty spectacular. The complaining and disagreeable couple got off in Durango, and Longarm was elated.

The other passenger was a gambler about Longarm's age who, upon discovering that he was riding with a United States marshal, grew sullen and distant. The man tossed down whiskey day and night from what seemed like a bottomless silver flask, but he never seemed to get completely drunk. He was well dressed and handsome, and Longarm had the feeling that he was probably either very lucky at cards or very cunning and adroit at cheating.

But finally, they came down into a wide valley where the high desert sage was more prevalent than pine trees. "Cortez is just ahead!" the driver shouted. "Cortez is comin' up!"

"Thank god," the gambler grumbled.

"Are you getting off here too?"

"No," the man replied sullenly. "But you are, so now maybe I can stretch out and have the entire coach to myself."

"How far are you going?"

"A long way."

"You strike me as a man who has a wanted poster out on him and someone that I probably should arrest and have locked up here in Cortez while they try to find out how many warrants are out on you."

"That would be a complete waste of the taxpayer's money . . . which from the looks of this settlement . . . isn't very much, as well as a complete waste of some local yokels' time."

Longarm had taken an instant dislike to this man, and he now realized that the feeling was mutual. And the gambler was probably correct. Putting him in the local jail on a suspicion was not a smart move and would waste time and money. Still, Longarm wasn't quite finished. "I'd bet my bottom dollar that you've seen the inside of many a jail."

The gambler extracted his silver flask, took a deep drink, then winked and said, "Have a nice stay in Cortez, Marshal Long."

"That's my full intention," Longarm told the man as the coach rolled to a stop in the little cattle community. "Play an honest hand and you'll never have to worry about the law again."

"Thanks for the fresh and very insightful advice," the gambler said, voice dripping with sarcasm.

Longarm had to suppress a strong urge to smash the man's face, but since he had more important considerations on his mind, he let the sarcasm pass and exited the coach.

You couldn't reason with someone like that gambler. He was smart, seemed educated, but he was as hard as the diamond on his finger. A man like that would continue marking his cards, dealing from the bottom of the deck, using devices that slipped cards from his sleeve into his hand, and double dealing.

"If I were you, I'd keep on going all the way to San Francisco," Longarm said, slamming the door shut.

"I'll keep that in mind."

The hell with it, Longarm thought, turning his back on the coach and the insolent gambler. If he played cards with the man, he was sure that he could catch him cheating within ten minutes. But the gambler was too cautious and too smart to play cards with a lawman, so he'd be free to ply his skills in another time and another place. But sooner or later, the odds would turn against him and someone would almost surely put a bullet through his hard and arrogant heart.

"Howdy! You need a room and some eats?" a heavyset man with a silver beard offered as he came to greet the incoming stage. "You the only one getting off here?"

"Afraid so. And who might you be?" Longarm asked.

He stuck out his hand. "Jake Beer, at your service. I own that little hotel across the street, and I have a very good Mexican cook that serves my boarders three excellent meals a day."

Longarm took a quick glance around Cortez. It was a pretty enough town, a little dry and dusty this summer, but still and all a nice community of perhaps a thousand people, most of them relying on the cattle trade, some logging, and a little silver and gold mining. The town hadn't grown much in the two years since he'd last passed through, but he'd always kind of liked it, and they said that

Cortez, being of lower elevation, was a fine year-round place for a man to hang his hat.

"How much do you get for a night's lodging?"

"Only one night?"

"I don't know," Longarm answered, stretching his limbs while the stage moved on down the street, where it would stop at a livery for a change of horses and drivers. "Maybe longer."

"What's your business in our fair town?"

"Not that it's any of your concern, Mr. Beer, but I'm looking for someone."

"Aren't we all," the man said with a wink and a chuckle. "Pretty young women!"

"Actually, that *is* what I'm looking for."

"I don't have any whores at my hotel, but there's a few over at Miss Maple's House. I don't allow them into the hotel because they're trouble. But Miss Maple has rooms to rent by the hour."

"I just came from Denver, and there are more whores there than a man could mount in six lifetimes," Longarm said. "I'm looking for a special woman who arrived here about two weeks ago. Redheaded woman. Tall, beautiful, and someone that you wouldn't forget."

"Oh, I didn't forget her," Beer said rolling his eyes. "Nobody would ever forget that face and figure."

"Is she in town?"

"She has come to town a couple of times with her brother, Robert Durham." Beer laughed. "Let me tell you something. When Mrs. Horton comes to shop in Cortez, everything stops. All the men stare, some of the married ones worse than the single, and behind corners or curtains. And the women . . . well, they stare too, but there is jealousy in their

hearts and no nice words to say behind Mrs. Horton's back.
No sir! The women of this town, including the whores at
Miss Maple's place, they just hate to see someone that beau-
tiful arrive. Makes the whores look ugly, she does."

"I need to see her."

Beer's big grin faded. "You a friend . . . or something?"

"Or something," Longarm replied, not wanting to di-
vulge his true purpose or identity. "Where can she be
found?"

"Why, at her ranch about five miles north of here."

"*Her* ranch?"

"Well," Beer said, "that's what the word is. Her brother
Robert runs it for her, but he doesn't know beans about
cattle, horses, or ranching. For that matter, neither does
Mrs. Horton. But they haven't bought any cattle yet, and
everyone has been trying to sell them beef for a big profit.
So far, they just haven't been interested in stocking their
ranch, which is one of the nicest around."

"Has Robert Durham been here long?"

"Hmmm, not very. About a year, I'd say. Yep, right at
a year. Nice fella, but quiet. Gets along with everyone but
doesn't say much about himself. Everyone wonders about
him, and it's clear that he's not from around here or even
from anywhere in the West. He has an Eastern accent. We
know that because plenty of Easterners come passin'
through on the stagecoach."

Longarm was dog tired, and although he would have
liked to rent a horse or buggy and go at once to see Lucy,
it sounded as if she was doing okay so far, so he decided
to put that off until tomorrow. He needed rest and a good
night's sleep.

"You say that your cook is good?"

"He's a prize. His tamales, enchiladas, beans and rice are as good as they get. He makes corn tortillas that are the best I've ever eaten. Trouble is you get pretty much the same thing morning, noon, and night."

"I can handle it," Longarm said. "And I'll take a room at least for tonight."

"Five dollars for the room, tonight's meal, and tomorrow's breakfast. You'll leave thinking it was money well spent."

"I'm sure that I will. Do Mrs. Horton and her brother come here on a regular basis?"

"You mean, like the same day every week?"

"That's exactly what I mean."

"I'm afraid not. Sometimes they come a couple of times a week, sometimes every other week. Mostly they buy groceries, and I've never seen them buy anything for livestock, like you'd expect from ranchers."

"Do they stay at your hotel?"

"Never. They'll eat a meal in town at the Cortez Café, do their shopping, and Robert will wet his whistle over at the Gay Lady Saloon for a little while waiting on his sister, then they're on their way back to the ranch."

"Anybody seem particularly close to them?"

Jake Beer paused and rubbed his face. "Seems to me that you're asking a lot of questions about Mrs. Horton and her brother. Mind if I ask why?"

"I don't mind at all," Longarm said. "But I'm not saying anything."

"We don't want trouble here. Mrs. Horton and her brother aren't well known in Cortez and they keep strictly to themselves, but people here have accepted them for what they are and we'd like to make sure that they're not bothered."

"I promise you, Jake, I'm not here to do them any harm. I know Mrs. Horton. We got to know each other in Denver. I'm her friend. I'm not saying it's anything more."

"And you're willing to take an oath on that part about it not being 'anything more'?"

"I won't take an oath on anything, but I hope you're not calling me a liar, Jake. That wouldn't sit too well with me."

"No, I'm not calling you a liar. I just . . . just have a feeling that there is a lot more here than meets the eye." The hotel owner smiled. "I'm sure you're tired after the long stagecoach journey, so let me take that valise and show you your room and the dining area."

The hotel was nice and it was clean. There were four rooms on the ground floor and the same number upstairs. Some of the hotel guests were already seated in the lobby and reading papers and carrying on conversations. Longarm could smell the rich aroma of chili and beef cooking in the kitchen. He doubted that he'd be staying long in Cortez, but this looked like a good place, where a man could be at ease and rest up. Also, if the cooking was as good as Jake Beer claimed, he would put on a few pounds, which was what his doctor had ordered.

"Too bad you're only staying for a night."

"I might stay longer. Just don't know yet."

"Meaning you have to talk to Mrs. Horton first to make your decision?"

Longarm almost laughed. "For a hotel owner, you sure do ask a lot of personal questions."

"Yeah," Jake Beer said, "I've always been a nosy bastard. My late wife, Gertie, she said I was the nosiest man she'd ever met and far worse than women when it came to gossip."

"And you didn't mind her saying that?"

"Hell no! I took it as flattery. Way I see it, if you don't ask about people and what they think and are up to, then you show you don't care about them. I ask, and my attitude is that if they don't want to answer . . . they won't. Like you with Mrs. Horton. I don't feel offended by that, just curious."

Longarm registered, was assigned room five at the top of the stairs, and took his key.

"Dinner is at six. I don't serve liquor, but I do sell it if you want wine or something stronger with your meal."

"I'll want a shot or two of whiskey. Maybe a beer with the Mexican food."

"I have good beer and whiskey. You'll be glad you stayed here, but I don't allow my guests to get drunk and rowdy at the table. Some do that and start arguments and then everyone gets riled up."

"I'll behave."

"I thought you would," Beer said. "Big as you are, you'd be a hell of a tough fella to *make* behave."

Longarm took his key, went upstairs, and looked at his room, the furnishings of which were far nicer than his own. He opened his window and looked down on the street.

Nice town, he thought, wondering how Lucy would react when he visited her tomorrow.

Chapter 8

After a Mexican supper that even exceeded Longarm's expectations, he decided to take a walk about the little town and see if he could gain any further insight or information about Lucy or her brother. He especially wanted to visit the Gay Lady Saloon and see what he could learn there.

The Gay Lady was a small establishment, even by Western standards, but what it lacked in size, it more than made up for in style. Instead of the expected tobacco-soaked sawdust on the floors, there was a fine hardwood floor polished and decorated with several large Navajo rugs. The bar glistened and the back bar was shiny with glasses and bottles, including some very expensive brands of liquor. Several big oil paintings adorned the walls, but by far the most prominent was one that depicted frolicking, almost naked women dancing on saloon tables while in the background a piano player pounded his keys with delight. The painting was about twelve feet long and six feet high, colorful and striking. One of the frolicking ladies bore a strong resemblance to Lucy Horton.

"Quite a work of art, wouldn't you say?" a blond and buxom woman in her early forties offered.

"Sure is," Longarm told her, shaking his head with amazement. "I've never seen anything like it."

"There was a painter from Europe. Ireland, to be exact, and his name was Patrick O'Toole. He came strolling into my place carrying an easel and a box of paints and brushes. Quite a handsome young fellow, and he wore a green derby hat and smoked a pipe with tobacco that smelled even more heavenly than French perfume. I liked the Irishman the minute I laid eyes upon him."

"And he offered to paint that picture?"

"Patrick was short of funds and very parched in the throat. He offered to paint my portrait for dinner, a girl for the night, and a bottle of my best whiskey. I have seen a lot of people who said they were talented artists who were terrible, so I said no."

"But the thirsty Irish artist persisted," Longarm guessed out loud.

"He did, and when he quickly sketched me with charcoal, I realized how very talented he actually was." The woman stuck out her hand. "My name is Molly Martin and I own this place."

"Pleased to meet you, Molly." Longarm returned his gaze to the painting. "Patrick O'Toole really did your establishment up fine. Is that you dancing on the second table to the right under the chandelier?"

"That's me without much more than my birthday suit on," Molly admitted, laughing. "Not bad, huh?"

Longarm clucked his tongue. "Not bad at all!"

"I told Patrick I wanted myself and my girls to look like

we were having a celebration . . . almost an orgy. We closed down this place for three straight nights while O'Toole painted and worked like a demon. And this is the result of his talent and effort."

"I hope you paid him well."

"Oh, I paid him *very* well because it isn't often you see genius walk right through your door. Patrick O'Toole had a big thirst and a big appetite for my girls, and I let him have his fill. And, if truth be known, he found *me* to be his favorite."

"I'll just bet he did," Longarm replied. "And what about that red-haired woman?"

"Oh, she is a beauty, that one! Do you recognize her?"

"I think she looks a lot like a lady I know."

The woman looked right into Longarm's eyes. "And that would be Mrs. Lucy Horton?"

Longarm blinked with surprise. "As a matter of fact, yes."

"Well, it *isn't* Lucy Horton, although a lot of people have told me that it is. I know better, however. The lady's name was Lizzy, and she came to Cortez with Robert Durham."

"Lucy Horton's brother?"

"That's right."

"Was Lizzy his and Mrs. Horton's sister?"

"I don't know. Lizzy was very secretive about her past. But I tell you this, when she had some liquor in her, she was a *wild* woman."

"Does she still live in Cortez?"

"Nope." Molly sighed. "She was found murdered less than two weeks ago. Someone strangled and very obviously raped and tortured her to death. Coroner here said that she suffered a great deal of pain before she was put out of her misery. She's buried in our local cemetery, and there are still some of the boys so smitten with the memory of her beauty that they lay flowers on her grave and they toast her in that painting and cry."

"Damn shame."

"Terrible shame." Molly's eyes turned hard. "I offered five hundred dollars reward to anyone who could help us catch Lizzy's murderer, but no one ever came up with a suspect."

"And you had no idea?"

"None at all," Molly replied. She forced herself to smile. "But let's not talk about the dead. Let's talk about us."

"*Us?*"

"Sure! What are we going to do next?"

"I thought I'd have a glass of whiskey then go back to the hotel and get a good night's sleep."

"You came in on the stagecoach today, and I saw you climb down and said to myself, 'Why, Molly, that is one big, handsome man. Wonder what he is doing in Cortez.' That's what I said to myself."

"Well, I'm here to see Mrs. Horton because we were friends in Denver."

"Real close friends?"

"Meaning?"

"Were you diddlin' her?"

Longarm felt his cheeks warm. "I'm a Southern gentleman, and we do not tell those kinds of secrets."

"Bravo for you!" Molly hooked his arm through her own and led him to the bar. She called down her bartender and ordered him to pour them two shots of her very best whiskey. "First shot to a gentleman in my Gay Lady Saloon is always on the house."

"Thank you!"

"My pleasure. Are you interested in having a woman tonight?"

"I . . . I think I'll probably pass on that pleasure, Molly."

"You don't look too poor to afford one of my girls."

"I'm just a bit under the weather."

"You're limping just a little. You've had some injuries, I take it?"

"I have."

Molly nodded. "You could use some more meat on those ribs, too."

"I expect that a few more Mexican meals at the hotel across the street where I'm staying will do the job."

Molly seemed to make a decision. She scooped up the bottle and led them over to a corner table, where she sat down and motioned Longarm to do the same. When they had drained their shot glasses, she refilled them and leaned closer. "You know something?"

"What?"

"I'm a very good judge of people . . . especially men. I can take in a stranger with a glance and almost always tell if he's got character or not. Tell if he's a snake or a charmer or a charlatan. A good man or a bad man or someone that is torn between the two with the Devil on one hand and Jesus on the other, each hollerin' in his ear to do their bidding."

"That's quite a valuable talent, Molly."

"It helps in my business. And the thing is that I instantly judged you to be a good man . . . and a *lawman*. So how is that?"

Longarm nearly choked on his whiskey. "All right, Molly, I *am* Deputy United States Marshal Custis Long and pleased to make your acquaintance."

They shook hands, Molly grinning. "So these questions you've been asking, they're really all about . . ."

"Mrs. Lucy Horton," he confessed. "I came here because twice back in Denver when we were out in public someone tried to kill her . . . or me . . . or us both."

"And that's how you got wounded and why you're limping?"

"That's right."

"What happened . . . exactly?"

Longarm leaned back in his chair. "If I tell you, you have to promise to keep what I say to yourself."

"I promise."

"And that I can drink more of this whiskey without paying for it, and the same goes for your company."

"Agreed."

"All right."

Longarm spent the next half hour telling Molly about what had happened in Denver and about what he knew of Lucy Horton's past back in Philadelphia and earlier in New Haven, Connecticut.

When he was finished, he leaned back in his chair and said, "Does what I just told you square with what you know about Lucy?"

"Actually, I don't know much at all about the woman. She never comes in here and we've barely spoken to each other. It's not that I get the impression she thinks that she's too good for someone like myself with a herd of whores. Nothing like that. I can tell when a so-called churchgoin' respectable woman lifts her nose in the air like I stink. But Lucy Horton was never anything but pleasant when we said hello in passing."

"What about her brother? I'm told that he often comes in here for a drink or two while his sister shops in town."

"Robert does. But he's about the quietest man I've ever known. Like his sister and your friend, he's pleasant enough, but he's made it clear to everyone that he isn't looking to make a friend or even have one of my girls. I've walked up to him and walked away a few minutes later feeling that my time would have been just as well spent talking to a cigar store wooden Indian."

Longarm had to smile. "I'm going to go out to their ranch tomorrow and see why Lucy never wrote me back and what is going on."

Molly patted Longarm on the sleeve. "My dear man, Lucy Horton is stunningly beautiful, but you may have to settle for the likes of me or one of my special girls. The woman might just have dumped you, Marshal."

"It wouldn't be the first time that has happened, but the thing is that Lucy's life could still be in danger. If someone tried to kill her twice in Denver, what reason do I have to suppose they'd not track her down to Cortez and attempt to finish the job?"

"None, I suppose."

"Well," Longarm said, "I just have to try to figure it all out and ask Lucy some hard questions."

"And if she refuses to answer or accept your help?"

Longarm had considered that possibility, that he'd come a long way for nothing. "If that is the way it goes, I'll just have to accept her decision and go back home."

"Stay awhile and rest up here in Cortez," Molly urged. "This is beautiful country. Are you a fisherman?"

"I dabble in it, but not too successfully."

"We have some great trout fishing, and if that doesn't appeal to you, we can do some sightseeing on horseback. Take a picnic out into a meadow someplace, and maybe have more than food for our pleasure."

Longarm grinned. "Molly Martin, are you trying to tempt me into sin?"

"Yep! Interested?"

"I could be."

"Depending on what Lucy Horton says and does tomorrow."

"You can almost read a man's mind, can't you?" Long-arm said. "You pretty much amaze me with your powers of observation."

"If you're amazed by them, wait until we have a private picnic by some mountain stream with some of the best wine that can be found between here and Denver."

Longarm tossed down some more whiskey just as a couple of Molly's girls appeared, along with the piano player, who looked just like he'd been painted in the big picture.

"You've quite a place here, Molly."

"Come back tomorrow and spend a little more time, Big Boy."

Longarm tipped his hat to the madam and headed for the door. If he stayed and had a few more whiskies, he'd wind up spending the night either with Molly Martin or one of her prettiest girls.

Chapter 9

Longarm rented a nice-looking buckskin mare at the Cortez Corral. The owner looked like an old Civil War veteran, and he had about as much personality as a wet blanket. "She's the best horse I have right now," the man assured him. "If you wanted to buy her, I'd have to ask fifty dollars and you'd be getting a bargain."

"I just want to rent a horse, not buy one."

"Suit yourself."

Longarm looked over at the corral. "I prefer geldings. Don't you have a good one to rent?"

"Nope. But don't you worry, mister. This horse will walk most any gelding into the ground. She's calm, sensible, and willing. She don't stumble, kick, or buck, and she can run like the wind if you need her speed."

"I don't expect to need to run her," Longarm said as the man saddled the mare and eyeballed the length of the stirrups. "Gonna have to let 'em out all the way or you'll be poppin' your chin with your knees."

"That sure as hell isn't much of a saddle you're putting on the mare," Longarm complained. "Most Indians ride better saddles. It looks like it's been thrown over the side of a cliff then roped and dragged a couple of hundred miles through rocks and brush."

"Hellfire, mister, I thought you said that you were only going to ride out to the Canyon Ranch! Ain't that far out and back, you know."

"I might want to do a little more riding. Why is the saddle horn bent on its side?"

"Some fool roped a buffalo and broke the saddle tree and snapped the horn. Don't matter much, does it? I mean, you sure don't look like a cowboy that is going to rope cows."

"It just looks stupid," Longarm said, beginning to dislike the man more and more.

"What it looks like don't matter if no one else sees you, and no one else is likely to see you ridin' out there today. And since you're bein' in a critical frame of mind, I ought to tell you that this fine mare was shod only last week and she'll ground tie. You just drop the reins in the dirt and she'll stand there until hell freezes over."

"She looks like a good animal," Longarm admitted. "But that old saddle appears to be about ready to fall completely apart."

"Well dammit!" the stable owner swore. "I could let you use my own saddle, but it'll cost you another fifty cents a day."

"I'll take it. And attach a pair of saddlebags to it so that I can take a few things."

"I'll do 'er. You want a rope, bullwhip, goat-hair chaps, or anything else as long as we're on the subject?"

Longarm knew the man was trying to be insulting, but

he ignored him and said, "A rifle and scabbard would be nice. But the rifle has to be a Winchester and it had better shoot straight."

"You planning to go deer hunting?"

"I might be."

"I got a Winchester you can borrow for another fifty cents a day plus the cost of the bullets."

"I'll take it along with a canteen with clean water."

The man glared at Longarm, but then he stomped off and brought back what was required.

Longarm checked the cinch, readjusted the stirrups on the old bastard's personal saddle, and inspected the rifle then rammed it into the saddle scabbard. "How much per day is all of this costing me?"

"Three dollars."

"You ought to have packed me a fine supper for that much money."

"Ride on out, and you'd better bring that mare back as sound as she is right now. If you lame her . . . you're gonna have to buy her!"

"Sure, sure," Longarm yelled over his shoulder as he set the mare into motion headed toward Lucy and her brother at the place that was known as the Canyon Ranch.

Longarm had no trouble following the directions he'd been given. There was a well-used dirt track leading out of town to the Canyon Ranch that would have been nearly impossible to miss. The ranch was backed up to a pine-topped mesa where a rushing stream fed down through the ranchland to the bottoms. The grass was high and green and it was nice country, which made it all the more puzzling why the Canyon Ranch wasn't stocked with grazing cattle.

The ranch house was made of logs and had a fine porch

facing to the west. The house was big, but not so big that it gave anyone the impression that the ranch was a large operation. Longarm's eyes took in the usual corrals, barns, and sheds, along with a few buckboards and wagons in various states of repair.

He pinned his eyes on the front door of the log house, and his heart was beating a little faster in the anticipation of seeing Lucy as he crossed the dirt yard and drew his horse up to a hitching post.

"Hello the house!"

There was no answer, and no one opened the door, so he tied the buckskin to a hitch rail and loosened her cinch. It was strangely quiet out here, and he guessed that Lucy and Robert had not bothered to adopt a ranch dog that would give them warning of company.

"Hello!"

Suddenly, Lucy came around from behind the house with a rifle clenched in her hands.

"Whoa!" Longarm shouted, throwing up his own hands. "Lucy, it's me, Custis!"

For a moment, he wasn't sure if she understood. And if she did recognize him, there wasn't a whole hell of a lot of happiness on her face.

"Custis?"

"Lucy, what. . . ."

She dropped the rifle and ran across the yard to throw herself into his arms. "Custis, I sure hoped that you'd come visit . . . but I didn't expect it."

"I kept waiting for your letter, but it never arrived."

"I'm sorry. Really sorry."

He held her tightly for a moment, felt her ribs and realized she'd lost a lot more weight than he had since they'd last been together.

"Lucy, what is going on here?" he asked, finally releasing her. "This place is deserted. And where is your brother?"

She stepped back and wiped her face. "Robert rode out yesterday and he hasn't come back. It's not like him to leave for the night. Did you see him in Cortez?"

"No. I was only there one night. He could have been in town, but I'm sure that someone would have pointed him out to me since I made no secret of the fact that I was coming out here to visit you both."

Lucy took his hands. "I'm worried sick about Robert. He said he'd found tracks out behind this house several mornings."

"Lucy," Longarm said, leading her over to the porch and gently placing her into a chair, then taking one for himself. "You'd better take a deep breath and start explaining what is going on here. Anyone could tell that something isn't right."

She interlaced her fingers together and squeezed her hands in her lap until her knuckles were white. "There's a lot to tell you, Custis."

"That sounds serious. Do you have any whiskey in the house before we start?"

"Sure. I'll get us some."

Longarm started to get up and follow the woman, but she shook her head, so he settled back into his chair and kicked his boot heels up on the porch rail. This sure was a nice little ranch, but something about it felt all wrong. He could see the worry . . . maybe even fear . . . in Lucy's eyes, and she was not a woman who spooked easily.

Lucy came back with two glasses, each holding two fingers of whiskey. "Here's to you, Custis," she said, raising her glass. "And to whatever may happen to us."

Longarm gave her a bewildered look, which she ignored as she drank, chin down.

"All right," Longarm said when it became clear that she was not going to start talking without some strong prompting, "let's just get to the meat of it. What *is* wrong here?"

"I think that someone might be watching us and that when Robert said that he found tracks out behind the house, they belonged to men that are waiting to . . . kill or rob us."

"What men?"

"I don't know."

Longarm shook his head. "Lucy, I've begun to suspect that you weren't entirely honest about everything you told me back in Denver. And once again I'm sure that now you know a whole lot more than you seem willing to tell me."

Lucy tossed down her whiskey and shook her head back and forth in silence.

Longarm was getting a little impatient and his voice roughened. "Dammit, woman, I can't help you out if I don't know what is going on. Are the same people that shot twice at you in Denver now stalking you and your brother here at the ranch?"

"I'm almost sure of it. After he found the tracks out back yesterday morning, Robert loaded a rifle and rode off to see if he could spot anyone that was out there . . . He didn't come back."

"That doesn't necessarily mean he's hurt or dead."

"I think that it does," Lucy argued. "Robert isn't one to sleep out in the woods. He . . . he's not the outdoor type. and he wouldn't shoot something to eat and build a campfire. No, Robert would hate staying out all night in the forest. He was afraid of things."

"Like the men he wanted to catch spying on you here at the ranch?"

"Yes. And of mountain lions and grizzly bears."

"They're not much of a worry anymore," Longarm assured her. "Most of the grizzly have been shot out in Colorado. Might be a few left, but they'd be rare and trying like hell to avoid humans. As for mountain lions, they'll watch a man and a camp . . . but from a great distance. Never known one to leap on a man before, and rarely even a horse. They've got plenty of deer up here to eat."

"I haven't heard any rifle shots," Lucy said. "I listened for them all afternoon yesterday and last night. None today either. If they got Robert, they're torturing him."

"Whoa!" Longarm exclaimed. "Why on earth would they capture and torture your brother?"

In reply, Lucy buried her beautiful face in her hands and began to cry.

Longarm tossed down his whiskey and got out of his chair to kneel down in front of the woman. "You know," he said in a gentle voice, "we've been shot at twice and we're not cats, so we can't possibly have nine lives. I'm thinking that you're just going to have to tell me what the hell is going on. Who is trying to kill you and who might have gotten your brother. If he really is your brother."

Her head snapped up. "Of course Robert is my brother! You don't think that . . . that he's my husband or lover or something like that, do you?"

"The thought has occurred to me."

"But I *slept* with you in Denver!"

"All right! Calm down. I believe you."

"Do you really?"

"I do about Robert being your brother. I can see by your

expression and the look in your eyes that he is your brother. But what else aren't you telling me, and why would you think that someone might even torture Robert?"

"Because they did it to Lizzy before they murdered her."

"Did you know Lizzy?"

"Yes. Back in Connecticut."

"Did she come out here with your brother?"

Lucy dipped her head. "She was wild, and they were supposed to stay here at the ranch, but you couldn't tie Lizzy down on an outpost like this ranch, so she stayed in town."

"And was strangled."

"That's what I heard. Robert was nearly overcome with grief. He wasn't the same afterward. When I arrived in Cortez, he'd fallen into a terrible state of depression. He didn't shave, didn't eat, and couldn't sleep."

"And no one ever found out who killed Lizzy?" Longarm asked.

"I think it's the same ones that have come out here at night and are stalking us."

"I see," Longarm said, although he didn't see at all.

Lucy pushed herself to her feet and grabbed a porch post for support. She spent several minutes staring at the mountains and then whispered, "It's beautiful out here, isn't it?"

"Yes, it is. This is really fine country and you've got a nice little ranch here. But no cattle. No dogs. No cowboys. What are you doing here, Lucy Horton? And is that *really* your name?"

"It is, I swear it is," she said, turning to face him.

"And what about the story concerning your late husband getting run over while racing a locomotive?" Longarm asked. "Is that also true?"

"Mostly."

"What does 'mostly' mean?"

"The truth is that *I* was driving the carriage, not Charles."

Longarm blinked. "You?"

"That's right. We had left a holiday party late in the day. As usual my husband was so drunk he couldn't stand, and I'd had to practically carry him out of the house we were visiting and lift him into the carriage. I didn't know how to drive the thing very well. I'd never done it before, but Charles was so drunk and he was in one of his vicious moods. He'd insulted the host and tried to corner the man's fifteen-year-old daughter in a bedroom. She'd fought him and screamed. People had rushed into the room, and they beat Charles and tossed him out. I was more humiliated than I've ever been in my life."

"So you got him into your carriage and he was cussing and fighting and you raced off," Longarm said, anxious to get to the end of this tragic tale.

"Yes. The horse was high-spirited. Green, they called it. Charles always bragged that he liked high-spirited animals and that was why he married me. But anyway, the horse was behaving as I drove the carriage away. Someone was yelling curses at Charles, and he twisted around and yelled back. A shot was fired."

"Someone at the party shot at you?"

"Everyone was drunk . . . but not as drunk as my husband, and no one there would ever have tried to rape a fifteen-year-old sweet and innocent young lady. There was a lot of anger when we left, and I just wanted to get out of there as fast as possible."

"So what happened next?"

Lucy threw up her hands in a gesture of utter helplessness. "When I heard the gunshot, I panicked. I slapped the reins down on the back of the horse, and it bolted and began to run. There was a railroad track a half mile down the road. I saw the train coming, but Charles didn't. He grabbed the buggy whip and started hitting the horse, and it went crazy running like the wind. The train blasted its horn at the road crossing. I knew we were going to die."

Lucy began to weep inconsolably. Longarm got up and took her into his arms. "And how did you survive?"

"I jumped! I saw what was going to happen and cried out for Charles to stop whipping the horse. He laughed and cursed me and then I jumped!"

"And the horse, carriage, and Charles were ground to pieces by the locomotive."

"Yes." Lucy shuddered. "I was spared the vision. When I jumped, I hit very hard and flipped over and over across the grass. I lost consciousness a split second before I heard a scream I'll never be able to forget."

"Charles."

"No, the poor horse. But they were both mutilated so badly that I later heard that . . . that it was all just blood, bone, and meat. Just one big mass of . . ."

Lucy lost control and could say no more.

Longarm held her closely. He knew that she could not say anything more about this horror today. Maybe not even tomorrow. And still, there was much that he had yet to learn.

Who was after this woman? Had the vengeful Horton family blamed her for the loss of their decadent son and brother? Had the rich family sent killers, or had maybe some of the younger ones even tracked Lucy to Denver themselves, planning to kill her?

The buckskin stood quietly as evening fell and the light

faded away. Longarm decided to take Lucy inside and put her to bed so she could get some sleep. He would take care of the mare and make sure that she had feed and water. And then he would wait and see if Robert returned to the Canyon Ranch.

Or not.

Chapter 10

Longarm sat up late that evening on Lucy's front porch, staring up at the stars and trying to figure out what was going on and what he might expect tomorrow when he saddled up the buckskin mare and went out to see if he could find Robert Durham. If he could believe that Lucy had finally told him everything and it was the truth, then it seemed pretty obvious that this was all about revenge.

He hadn't come from a wealthy or influential family himself, but he'd known quite a few in his time, both when he grew up in West Virginia and then during and after the Civil War. Later in life he'd crossed swords with some pretty important people during his years as a United States deputy marshal, and he'd come to the conclusion that people with money and power often believed that they could write all their own rules. It would not matter to the Horton family that Charles had been a drunken and abusive man or even that he'd tried to rape a child. No, that would not matter at all. The Horton family would blame anyone not of their own blood, and in this case that blame would fall on Lucy and her brother.

It all made perfectly good sense. But something . . . something that Longarm could not quite put his finger on was missing. Some small piece of information that would fully explain to his own satisfaction exactly what was going on here in Colorado.

And then about midnight, it came to him like a blazing star across the dark sky. *Money!* There was money involved somehow, and that was what Lucy was not telling him.

Was she due to inherit a widow's fortune? Was there a last will and testament that gave her a great deal of money? If so, where was it and how was it to be implemented?

Longarm didn't know the answer to that question, but he vowed he would drag it out of Lucy tomorrow. What she had to understand was that he couldn't really protect her unless he knew the rules of this vengeful, murderous game being played.

They both slept a little later than expected, and the sun was well up in the eastern sky when Longarm plodded into the kitchen to find Lucy sipping a cup of hot coffee while stirring some fried potatoes and pork.

"Sorry, we don't have any chickens, so there are no eggs," she said, forcing a smile as she worked at the stove. "Eggs in Cortez are very expensive, and it's nearly impossible to get out here without breaking at least half."

"I'll be fine with whatever you're cooking, Lucy. How about some coffee?"

"Hope you like it strong and black."

"I do."

They ate a hearty breakfast, and when it was finished, Longarm said, "We need to talk about Robert."

"What do you need to know about my brother?"

"Why did he come out here?"

"He was afraid of the Horton men. He was, in that family's eyes, guilty by association. They had whipped him several times, and he was deathly afraid of them all. My brother didn't have any money, so I gave him enough to get out of Philadelphia."

"To come to this ranch."

"Yes."

Longarm drank his coffee and found it to his liking. "And now the real question. How did you come to own this ranch, Lucy?"

"I bought it."

"With?"

"Money."

"Which came from where?" Longarm pressed. "Lucy, dammit, you've got to come clean with me or I can't help you!"

"More coffee?" she asked, starting to get up and go over to the stove.

Longarm grabbed her arm and forced her none too gently back down in her chair. "Where did you get the money to buy this fine ranch? Judging by the grass, fencing, house, and outbuildings, it didn't come cheap."

She sighed. "What if I told you I got the money from my own family in New Haven, Connecticut?"

"I don't think that I'd believe you."

"All right, I didn't. I got it from the Horton family just before I left Philadelphia."

"As part of a will?"

"Charles never got around to having a will prepared," Lucy said bitterly. "So I was left out in the cold. With nothing."

"But that wasn't fair, was it?" Longarm said quietly as he noted the fury in her eyes. "Not fair at all."

"No!" She lowered her voice. "Of course not. He'd promised to always see that I had money. I'd suffered that mean, drunken monster for a long time, and I felt that I deserved to be well repaid."

"But the Horton family felt otherwise."

"Of course they did." Lucy took a deep breath. "The patriarch of the family told me that as far as he was concerned I was nothing and would get nothing. That I was responsible for the death of his son when that train struck our carriage, and he would never, ever forgive me."

"What did you say and do?" Longarm asked.

"I told the old tyrant that he owed me plenty. That I wasn't going to leave Philadelphia without a fair settlement. I even had a figure that I'd written on a piece of paper, and I gave it to him. I told him that I'd earned every penny of it many times over."

"How much?"

"Forty thousand dollars," Lucy replied. "Not much really, considering what I'd been subjected to by Charles. And the family was worth several million dollars. I thought the figure was more than fair, but the old man just laughed and threw the paper back into my face."

"Did you hurt or kill him?"

Lucy's jaw dropped. "What?"

"You heard me."

"No!"

"But you managed to find a way to get what you thought was a fair compensation despite the old man's reaction."

She nodded her head with satisfaction. "Yes, I did."

"How?"

"I emptied my husband's account before they could get their greedy hands on it. I sold my household silverware and art . . . valuable art. I sold some other things, like my diamond wedding ring and a pearl necklace. There was jade and some emeralds too. I sold everything that I could find and take from our house in a hurry."

"And while you were doing that, you told Robert to buy you a ranch in some remote place in Colorado. A pretty ranch and don't worry about stocking it with cattle."

"How did you guess?"

"Not too hard." Longarm took a sip of coffee, his mind working the most likely way this had unfolded. "So your brother bought this ranch with the money you were able to grab and send."

"That's right. And I went into hiding for a short time and then came to Denver."

"Why didn't you come straight here to join your brother?"

"I wanted to . . . until we met. The reason I decided to stay awhile in Denver was to see if they'd found my track west and had found me. The very last thing I wanted was for them to come here and hurt or kill my poor brother."

"Where is all the money now?"

"In this ranch."

"I don't believe it," Longarm said. "From what little you've said, you have to have a lot more money hidden somewhere."

Lucy shook her head. "That is my secret, Custis, and my secret it will remain."

"Even if it is the cause of Lizzy's death, possibly followed by Robert's death and your own?"

Lucy bowed her head. "Custis, I know that to a lawman I must look like a greedy thief. But I only took what was coming to me. Charles lied about most everything, and he even showed me a draft of his last will and testament. He said that he had it notarized and recorded . . . but he didn't. The draft that I had was never finalized, and Charles had no intention of ever doing so. What I took was what was in *my* household. My own jewelry and property and our bank accounts. Is there anything illegal or immoral about that?"

Longarm carefully considered the question. "If what you say is true, then no judge or jury would find you guilty. But . . . and this is very important . . . what you did probably got Lizzy murdered, and it might have already gotten your brother the same."

"I know that!" She scrubbed bitter tears from her eyes. "Why can't that family be content to just wallow in its wealth and leave me alone? Why do they have to come so far and be so horrible?"

"My guess is that they didn't leave Philadelphia. People that rich hire other people to do their dirty work. I think that the Horton family has hired assassins that will not stop until they have everything you own in their grasp."

"Then what hope is there?"

"There's always hope," Longarm told her. "I'm going out this morning and try to find your brother. I'm a pretty good tracker, and believe me I know how to read signs of violence. If your brother is still alive, I'll find and bring him back here."

"Oh, thank you!" Lucy cried, jumping up and hugging his neck.

"You're welcome. But even if Robert is still alive, that

won't take away the threat. People like the Horton family don't pay assassins to fail."

"So they won't give up."

"No," Longarm said, "they won't. And even if I kill the ones that are in Colorado, there's every possibility that more will be hired."

"Then . . ."

"I might have to go to Philadelphia or find a way to draw them to Colorado," Longarm explained. "I just don't see any other way out of this death hunt."

"Be careful out there, Custis."

"I will be. And you should arm yourself and lock the doors until I return. Don't let anyone inside even if they look completely harmless."

"All right."

Longarm got up from the table, kissed Lucy, and found his coat, gun, and hat. He made sure that the Winchester he'd rented was loaded and in proper working order, and then he trudged out to the barn and saddled the buckskin mare. He was going to start hunting for Robert Durham, but he had a sick feeling in the pit of his stomach that he would find nothing but a disfigured and tortured carcass bearing little resemblance to a human being.

Chapter 11

Longarm rode out of the ranch yard with the buckskin mare tossing her head and acting as if she was ready to go somewhere far away.

"Ease up there, girl. What we need to do is to start riding circles around this ranch house and see if we can pick up some sign. "There hasn't been any rain in the last few days, and it shouldn't be too hard to come upon some fresh tracks."

Longarm was right. He found some hoofprints leading off to the north, and they were stamped over some other tracks. He quickly realized that Robert Durham's mount wasn't shod but that the horses he followed were shod, and he tucked that valuable piece of information away to be used later.

The tracks led off the ranch property and straight up through some rocky hills where the tracking was more difficult. Several times Longarm had to dismount and look very close to see places where the iron shoes of horses had

chipped at the hard rock. Once, he found the butt of a cigarette burned down to a nub. Longarm put the cigarette butt
into his vest pocket and kept covering ground. Where the
terrain permitted, he loped the mare, and where it was too
rough, he put her into a ground-eating trot.

The day grew warm, and yet it was pleasant out because
there was a gentle breeze. Longarm looked often to the
sky, expecting to see turkey vultures circling above, but
they never appeared.

And then, about one o'clock in the afternoon, he came
upon a place where there had been an ambush. He dis-
mounted and dropped his reins, trusting that the mare really was trained to ground tie and would not go running
all the way back to Cortez.

Longarm found empty shell casings and also signs in
the dirt of a fierce struggle. Even more ominous, he found
dried bloodstains on the rocks and grass. But what he
didn't find was Robert Durham's body.

Taking his time, he circled the area reading everything
he could from the marks left behind. Longarm was not a
professional tracker, but it didn't take one to see that there
had been a fight here that involved more than two men.
The boot marks and the shod hoofprints he was reading
indicated that Robert had been shot, wounded, but had
fought at least three attackers until he was either killed or
captured and taken away.

"I don't give him much hope," Longarm said to the
mare as he climbed back into his saddle and followed
the tracks down into a narrow valley that ran to the southwest.

Longarm drew his horse up and leaned forward, weight
resting on his saddle horn. He had an important decision
to make, and it was one that could not wait.

Should I go on without food, blankets, or much ammunition . . . or should I return to the Canyon Ranch and get Lucy to provision me? And if I leave her there, will she be in danger or is all the danger in front of me someplace?

Longarm wanted to go straight forward. To put the buckskin mare into a high lope and try to overtake the ones that had either killed or captured Robert Durham. But another part of his brain said that the man was probably already dead and that his first concern ought to be for Lucy.

So, with some reluctance, Longarm turned the mare back toward Canyon Ranch and made her show how fast she could really run.

Lucy was standing out in the yard and had seen him coming for a long time. Her beautiful face revealed her dread, and as soon as Longarm drew the mare up at the hitch rail, she rushed over to him.

"Did you find Robert?"

"No, but I found where he was attacked."

"Was he . . ."

"He was taken away by at least three men and I don't know if he was alive at that point . . . or dead."

Lucy wrung her hands. "We've got to find out one way or the other. If he's alive, we have to save him. If he's dead, we have to bury him!"

"I know." Longarm took Lucy's hands into his own. "They may be within ten miles of us and they may be a hundred miles away. If they're close, I could have gone on, but there was just no way of knowing. So what we need to do is to prepare for a long manhunt."

"How long?"

"As long as it takes to find your brother dead or alive. And as long as it takes for me to either capture or kill whoever got him."

"All right," she said, looking back over her shoulder at the house. "I've got food I can pack. Canteens and grain for the horses. I have blankets and other things."

"We can't take a pack animal even if you have one."

"I don't," she admitted. "There were only two horses on the place, and we used the one I ride to pull the buckboard back and forth to Cortez when we went for supplies."

"But you do have a saddle for that animal and can ride it?"

"Of course."

"Then I'll saddle the horse you have left while you pack whatever we can tie behind our cantles."

"This is going to be rough," she said. "But we have to find Robert."

Longarm nodded. "If the weather holds good, we can make excellent time and I can follow their tracks without much trouble. They were heading southwest."

"That would be toward the Arizona Territory and Navajo Indian country."

"That's right. Rough country without a lot of water. But I've dealt with the Navajo plenty of times and even have some friends on their reservation. You needn't be worried about them killing and scalping us, Lucy. We'll be all right among those people."

"I hope so."

"I'm just not sure why the ones who attacked your brother would head out that way."

"Only one way to find out," Lucy said. "I'll get to packing. We ought to be able to ride for another three or four hours before dark."

"It's going to be a tough chase," Longarm told the woman. "If you have a rifle and ammunition, that would be good."

"I can shoot," she told him. "It was one of the few things that Charles could do well. And he taught me how to shoot clay pigeons."

"What we're after are a lot harder to hit than clay pigeons," Longarm promised. "We could get ourselves killed."

Lucy stopped on the way to the house and turned to face him. "I couldn't live with the fact that what I did caused another death. Lizzy was not the kind of woman that I cared much for . . . but she didn't deserve what she got. I'll do anything to keep Robert from suffering the same fate."

"I know."

Longarm spun on his heel and headed for the barn. He had hardly noticed a horse in one of the stalls, and he hoped it was a strong and fast animal and would not give out after a few hours of hard riding. And he hoped the same was true of Lucy Horton.

Chapter 12

They camped by the San Juan River on their first night out, and not much was said between them because of their concern about the fate of Robert Durham.

Longarm made a cooking fire down in a deep dry wash where they had tied their horses. And afterward, he thought there was some awkwardness between them because Lucy still hadn't quite told him the entire story.

"Is there a fortune hidden on your Canyon Ranch property?" he asked as their small campfire died down. "Is that why the three we are after might have kept Robert alive?"

"He doesn't know a thing," she said quietly. "But yes, there are some diamonds and precious stones that I have kept for stocking the ranch or for an emergency. And they are very valuable."

"If they torture your brother, that's what they're trying to find out," Longarm told her. "And if he really doesn't know anything, they'll keep torturing Robert until he is dead."

Lucy got up from beside the fire. "Let's just try to make better time tomorrow and overtake them."

"Your horse is willing, but it isn't a very good animal and it's slowing me down. On the buckskin mare, I can make a lot better time."

She looked at him intently. "Custis, are you suggesting that I return to the ranch?"

"Yeah, I am."

"Well I'm not going to do that!" Lucy proclaimed. "I'll push my pony harder tomorrow."

"You could kill him trying to keep up with me."

"I'll keep up."

"You're not a good rider, and you've probably got saddle sores all over your pretty bottom and on your lovely thighs."

For the first time all day, Lucy smiled. "And I suppose the next thing you're going to suggest is that I have you examine and medicate them."

"Wouldn't be such a bad idea . . . if I had some salve . . . which I don't."

"Then I guess my butt and thighs are just going to have to suffer for a while longer, huh?"

Longarm took a slug of whiskey. "If you return to the ranch, I will bring Robert back dead or alive. That's my promise, Lucy."

"Let's not talk about this anymore. How old are the tracks now?"

"Eight hours maybe."

"Are we still following four horses?"

"Yep."

"That means that my brother is alive."

"Not necessarily," Longarm told her. "Robert might be dead and draped across his saddle."

Lucy's expression darkened. "I'm going to sleep, Custis. Whichever one of us wakes first needs to rouse the other so we can get a very early start."

"Good idea. Even though I've always gotten along well with Navajo, there are some renegades, and they'd like nothing better than to kill us and take our horses and provisions. That being the case, the sooner we are off their reservation the easier I'll feel in my mind."

Lucy came over to Longarm and kissed him. "Thanks for risking your life to save that of someone you don't even know. You didn't have to do this."

"Yes, I did. I'd do it even if Robert wasn't your brother. I'd do it because a man has been taken by force. Based on what happened to Lizzy, we know that they won't hesitate to torture your brother."

Lucy kissed him a second time, and then she rolled up in her blankets and instantly went to sleep. Longarm watched her and the stars for about another twenty minutes, and when he realized his eyes were starting to lose focus, he scooped out a little sleeping cradle in the river bottom sand and went to sleep under his own blankets.

The sun was lifting off the horizon when Lucy and Longarm tightened their cinches and rode out of the dry wash following their quarry. And with each passing hour Longarm felt more hope that Robert Durham was still alive. He was probably being starved and denied water, but a man could take that for three or four days if the sun wasn't too hot.

"Look," Longarm said, pointing. "Do you see that little rooster tail of dust way down to the southwest?"

Lucy squinted. "I believe that I do."

"It's probably them," Longarm told her.

"How far ahead of us are they?"

"Four . . . maybe five miles is all. From this point on we're going to have to be a bit more careful not to be seen. We're outnumbered, and our best hope of saving your brother's life is to attack when they are least expecting it."

"How are we going to do that out in this open, brushy country?"

"There are lots of rocks and hillocks," Longarm told her. "And we'll use them all to close in on that bunch. Maybe they'll stop at noon and take a little siesta. If they do and we can get into firing range, we'll open up and try to either kill them or drive them away from your brother."

"And that's the best that you can come up with?"

"At the moment. But if you have a better idea, then I'd like to hear it."

"I think we should split up and both ride a big loop around them so that we are ahead of them when they see us. If we do that, they're not going to think we're from Cortez and they'll be easier to kill."

"Not a bad plan, but they're almost sure to see one or the other of us, and besides, I don't think your horse could get around in front of them."

Lucy patted the little bay that she was riding. "He's a scrub, all right. And I'm sure that he's pretty old. I really don't want to punish him any more than I have to."

"Let's just keep following them. I'm thinking we can wait until they camp and fall asleep, then slip in and get your brother out of their grasp before they even know what happened."

"I sure do hope that works."

"It has to work," Longarm said dryly.

* * *

It was two hours after dark and the campfire up ahead was dying, telling Longarm that he and Lucy had to start moving. "It's about a half mile to their camp. Let's tie our horses and go the rest of the way on foot. The wind is in our faces, so we caught a break. If it were to our backs blowing toward their camp, their horses would pick up the scent and they could start whinnying, which would be disastrous."

Longarm checked his Winchester and turned to Lucy. "It would be better if you had a rifle, but that double-barreled shotgun is going to be damned effective if we get in close. Just make sure that you don't wind up blowing your brother or me to pieces."

"I've got a pistol in my waistband," she said. "But I'm no good with one. Maybe they'll just throw up their hands and you can arrest them."

"Wouldn't count on it," Longarm told her. "Let's go. Follow me in single file, and I don't have to tell you that we must be silent."

"No, you don't."

Longarm struck out on foot. After two days in the saddle, he didn't mind the walking, but he wished that the moon wasn't so bright. He figured that an almost full moon was both an advantage and a disadvantage. It was an advantage because it ought to allow them to make sure they didn't accidentally shoot Robert Durham. But it also increased their chances of being seen before they were in a good firing position.

He glanced over his shoulder at Lucy. She was clutching the shotgun, and he knew both hammers were cocked, so he hoped that she wouldn't trip over a rock or anything and give him both loads in the back.

When they got close, Longarm dropped to his hands and knees, and since the sagebrush was thick, he was no longer silhouetted against the high desert night sky. Lucy did the same.

He crawled within fifty feet of the camp and saw that two of the men were still sitting up talking and sucking on a bottle of whiskey.

"You might have already killed the tenderfoot son of a bitch," one of the men said. "He can't take much more of this."

"I know. In the morning we'll start putting his feet to our campfire. Pour hot coals over 'em, and if that doesn't do it, I'll drop burning embers on his face. He'll talk, by gawd. He'll talk or I'll burn him alive!"

"Can't say that I'm looking forward to watching that," the other man said. "I heard of Apache tying white captives to a wagon's wheel and burning them alive. This seems even worse and one helluva lot slower."

"Durham should have spilled his guts right away and saved us all this misery."

"Maybe he really doesn't know where the Horton diamonds and jewelry are hidden."

"He knows! How couldn't he know? And he's gonna tell us in the morning before we slit his damned throat or watch his head go up like a torch."

Longarm heard a small choking sound and turned to stare at Lucy. He whispered, "Get that scattergun up and ready, but don't use it unless I yell for you to pull both triggers."

"I'm not sure which one is Robert. They're both too far from the firelight to tell."

"He'll be the one with the rope around his boot tops," Longarm said. "See him?"

She stared then nodded.

"I'm going in and you just back me up, Lucy."

Longarm crawled fast toward the campfire, and when a horse swung its head in his direction and snorted, pulling against the picket line, the two drinking partners swiveled around to see what was spooking the animal.

"Freeze!" Longarm shouted, coming to his feet with the rifle at his shoulder.

One of the men went for his gun, and Longarm shot him in the chest, knocking his body into the campfire. The other man tried to tear his gun from his holster, and that gave Longarm little choice but to shoot him in the belly. The fatally wounded man collapsed screaming at the top of his lungs.

The third man, who had been asleep in his blankets, jumped up and dove into the brush. Longarm got a shot off at him, and then Lucy ran forward and emptied both barrels of her big shotgun. Brush was torn apart, and Longarm heard a howl of pain.

"Come on out of there!"

"Don't kill me!"

Robert groaned and tried to sit up. Lucy dropped the shotgun and ran to his side.

Longarm knew that he had a wounded man out in the brush, and he didn't know if that man was armed or not. Probably was armed, or at least that was the smart way to be thinking.

He moved in the direction that he'd seen the man disappear, crouching and trying to keep from getting ambushed in the semidarkness. A wounded man was like a badly wounded animal in that the wounding often made him all the more desperate and dangerous.

"You might as well stand up and reach for the stars,"

Longarm said quietly. "You aren't going anywhere out here. If I don't find you tonight, I'll track you down first light in the morning."

There was a long silence and then a sob. "I'm hit real bad, mister. Shotgun near tore off my shoulder and I'm bleedin' something awful!"

"You better throw your hands up and start toward me, or I'll let you bleed to death out in the brush."

"You're going to finish me," the man wailed. "If I stand up where you can see me, you'll shoot me in the head!"

"I guess you don't have much in the way of choices. Is that man that you were torturing going to live?"

"He should. Jeb was going to torch him in the morning if he wouldn't tell us what we had to know. But he was alive when he went down, and it was me that covered him with a blanket!"

"Well aren't you the sainted one?" Longarm replied. "Stand up or bleed out. Makes no difference to me."

"Okay. I'm standing up with my hands over my head. Please don't shoot."

Longarm thought a man who was part of torturing a woman deserved a slower death than to be shot in the head, but he didn't say that to this whimpering snake.

The man rose out of the brush, and Longarm could see that he was young and tall. He had long hair, a full beard, and his face was bloody.

"Come toward me," Longarm ordered.

The man walked toward Longarm, who asked, "What is your name?"

"George."

"George what?"

"George Hall. And I wasn't even in Cortez when Jeb

and Art killed and raped that woman outside the Gay Lady Saloon. I swear that I wasn't!"

"Sure."

"Who are you?" the man blurted.

"I'm a federal marshal and . . . if you don't bleed out, I'll take you to Cortez, where you'll surely hang by the neck."

"But I didn't kill that woman and I wasn't doing anything to hurt Mr. Durham."

"Of course I believe that you were just along for the ride, George. Now, let's get back to the camp. You armed?"

"No. I swear it!"

"If I find out you're lying, I'll put your face in the fire and watch your hair burn and sizzle."

"Oh gawd!"

George nearly fell over, but Longarm grabbed him by the arm and shoved him back toward the campfire.

"Lucy, how is your brother?" he asked.

"Nearly dead." Her eyes blazed, and she took the pistol from her waistband and started toward George, cocking back the hammer. When the tall young outlaw saw her coming at him, he tried to turn and run back into the brush screaming.

"No!" Longarm shouted, tackling Lucy and tearing the gun from her hand.

"Let go of me! He's going to get away again!"

Longarm stood up. "You hit George Hall pretty good with that scattergun, Lucy. He's bleeding badly and I don't think he can run fifty feet without collapsing."

"Then let him go and die where I don't have to see him suffer!"

George fell to his knees and turned around toward the

campfire. "You might as well let her shoot me dead as try and keep me alive for the hangman's rope. Go ahead, Mrs. Horton, put a bullet in my head. It's what I deserve."

Lucy said something under her breath and went back to attend to her brother. Longarm knelt over Robert and examined him as well as he could in the firelight. "Robert, are you shot or stabbed?"

"No," the man whispered. "I'm hurt and I need water!"

Lucy ran to get a canteen. "Where are you hurt?" Longarm asked.

"The pair of men you just shot and killed sure kicked the hell out of me. Broke some ribs and my arm."

"They didn't do a bad job on your face, either," Longarm observed, noting the cuts and severe swelling around the man's eyes and how his nose had been broken. "But you still might make it."

"Water, please."

Lucy gave her brother water and then bathed his battered face with a rag. Robert moaned and tried to sit up, but they kept him lying down.

"Don't let him drink too much all at once," Longarm warned. "Just a few sips to start, then more through the night."

"Is he . . ."

"I'm no doctor and your brother is busted up pretty good, but he says that he hasn't been shot or stabbed, so I'd put money on him pulling through this if we can get him some doctoring."

"Custis, we both know that the nearest doctor is in Cortez."

"You're right," Longarm agreed. "But maybe I can find someone that will help save him right here among the Navajo."

"Like . . . like a medicine man?"

"Or a medicine woman," Longarm told her. "Either one would do. They have herbs and poultices and medicines that work damn well. I've been a patient of a medicine man and he saved my life."

"But where could you find one way out here in the middle of . . . of nothing?"

Longarm thought that was a good question. He looked over at George Hall, who was on his knees rocking back and forth and leaking like a sieve. George was in worse shape than Robert Durham, and it was doubtful he'd make it through the night. And why should the man even try if he was going to hang?

"We'll see what the morning will bring, Lucy. If your brother lives through the night . . . and I expect he will . . . we'll find a Navajo that knows medicine."

"And what about him!" she spat, jabbing a finger in George Hall's direction. "What if he makes it through the night? Are you going to ask a Navajo to try and save that murderer?"

"Not likely," Longarm answered. "But I sure do have some questions for George to answer. Don't you think that you'd like to hear what he has to say about who sent him and those other two murdering bastards?"

"I think I already know all the answers."

"Well, maybe you do, but I'm a federal officer of the law and I want to hear a confession with my own ears. If I get George to tell us all about this business, I can go back to Denver and get a judge to sign a warrant to arrest whoever paid these men with blood money."

Lucy nodded with understanding. "You'd better talk fast to that son of a bitch, because I think I blew half of his shoulder off and he looks ready to go straight to hell."

"I expect that's true," Longarm agreed as he went over to George and said, "Come sit by the fire and maybe some whiskey will help."

"I'd sure like some whiskey."

Longarm picked up the bottle. It had landed just right, and although uncorked, it still held a good many swallows. "It's all yours, George, if you start talking."

He was fighting not to lose consciousness. "I'm a dead man, aren't I?"

"I'm afraid so."

"I didn't want to get into this awful business. They forced me to be a part of it."

"Were you one of the men who tried to kill me and Lucy Horton over in Denver?"

"No, I'm from Cortez. I never even got away from these parts to see Denver."

Longarm gave the kid the bottle. "Drink 'er down, but tell me everything I want to know."

"I'll try." George raised the bottle and choked down a slug. He bowed his head and wept then blubbered, "It started at the Gay Lady Saloon when I fell in love with Lizzy, and I think she cottoned up to me."

Longarm could believe that. The young man was really quite handsome had he been washed, his hair cut, and his beard trimmed. "So what happened?"

"I saw Jed and Bert grab her and take her away after the saloon closed. I followed them and tried to help Lizzy, but I couldn't do nothin' to save her. They put a gun to my head and told me they'd blow my brains out if I didn't throw in with them and go out to that ranch."

"Mrs. Horton's Canyon Ranch?"

"That's right. I didn't even know why! But after what

they did to poor Lizzy, I knew I was going to die if I didn't go along. So I did."

Longarm shook his head with disgust. "You were sweet on Lizzy, and they raped and strangled her, and you weren't man enough to try to get even?"

"I . . . I wasn't."

"George, you sure enough deserve to hang, but I just don't think that you're going to get the chance, because you're dying."

"I know. I'll go to hell too. I know that I'll go to hell."

"Did Robert Durham tell you where the diamonds and jewelry are hidden at the ranch?"

George drank again; his voice was fading and he was hard to hear. His head kept falling to his chest and his breathing was loud and labored.

"I don't think he knew . . ."

George tried to say more, but he keeled over and heaved his last sigh.

Longarm stared at the young man's body. Maybe George had told the truth at the last and really had no choice but to go along with Jeb and the other man that Longarm had killed by the campfire.

Maybe, but Longarm doubted it.

Chapter 13

"There's a big storm brewing," Longarm said at sunrise. "I can see thunderheads coming at us from the west. We could weather a cold rainstorm, but your brother wouldn't survive."

Lucy had also seen the dark clouds building on the horizon. "So what are we going to do?"

"There's no time to bury the dead, and after what they did to Lizzy and your brother, they don't deserve burial. We've got their three horses plus the one that Robert was riding. That gives us a total of six horses. Your bay is by far the slowest and weakest, so we'll leave him here and ride the five, moving as fast as we can trying to outrun the storm."

"How can Robert sit a saddle in his awful condition?"

"I don't know, but if we are overtaken by a storm, it would most likely be his death sentence."

"But . . ."

Longarm placed his arms on her shoulders. "Lucy, this

is a hard deal all the way around. Especially for your brother, but if he's lived this long, he may be tougher than he appears. The best that we can do is just to head on back toward Cortez and hope we can find shelter and medicine."

She took a deep breath. "You don't deserve to have this burden, Custis. If I hadn't taken what I did from the Horton family, none of this would have happened."

"That's water under the bridge. And besides, it sounds to me like what you did was completely justified. You were promised things that would be spelled out in a will, but your late husband lied, and then his family cast you out the door without a cent."

"Thank you for understanding. We'll do our best to hurry, because I agree that those storm clouds look threatening. So outrunning them seems like our best choice."

"Right now," Longarm said, "it's really our *only* choice."

Just before she started to get busy, Lucy said, "I'll never forgive myself if Robert dies before we can get him help."

"This is no time for regrets. Pack our things while I saddle the buckskin mare and all of the other horses. I'll take the dead men's weapons and anything else I can find that might help us along the way back to Cortez. There is no time to waste."

"I'm not hopeful about finding help between here and Cortez. We didn't see a soul since leaving the ranch. No homesteads. Nothing."

"We were following tracks to overtake your brother. On the way back to your ranch, we'll take a different trail . . . one more direct and that will give us a better chance to find help."

"All right," she said. "I'll wake Robert up and tell him why we have to move him."

"Listen," Longarm said. "You hear the faint rumble of thunder?"

"I do."

"Let's move!"

They tied Robert Durham to his saddle, and Longarm told Lucy that she might have to ride up behind the man to hold him upright.

"I can hang on by myself," Robert said, his face as pale as fresh snow. "I know I look like a dead man, but I've got something left in me."

Hearing those words meant a lot to both Lucy and Longarm. Lucy might have known her brother had some grit, but until he'd heard Robert speak, Longarm had figured the Easterner was a weakling and as good as dead, that Robert would never hold up to additional punishment and would just fall off his horse, refuse to move, and then die.

"I'll ride close to you," Longarm offered, tying a rope to the extra saddled horses. "Lucy, you ride on the other side of Robert's horse, and between the two of us we'll keep him in the saddle."

Robert managed a weak grin. "Sorry to be so much trouble."

"You'll do to ride the trail with," Longarm said, not trying to hide his admiration, because although this man was slight, he was a fighter.

They tried to gallop but quickly found that would not do, because even Lucy, who was not a horsewoman, was having trouble, and Robert was in agony and swaying like a drunken sailor trying to reach the wharf where his ship was tied.

"We'll try the jog," Longarm decided. "A nice, easy jog."

But the jog was really a rough trot, and when Robert almost fell, Longarm reined his horse in and said, "We're going to have to go at the walk and just hope we can find shelter before we're overtaken by the storm."

And that's what they did. They rode straight for the Canyon Ranch, and after a while they managed to ignore the hard, cold, and pushing wind that Longarm knew was just ahead of a chill and driving rain. This was high desert country and not given to much rain, but when it did come, it usually came down in torrents, turning dry washes into raging creeks that would be impossible to cross.

By noon they were approaching a long, broken ridge of red mesas to the east. Longarm was hoping that maybe there were some caves that they could hole up in for the rest of the day and night. He was hoping that he'd have time to gather some dry wood, mesquite, or even some dead branches off a piñon pine.

"Look!" Lucy cried. "A trail of smoke!"

Longarm saw it then, and when he squinted hard, he could see that there were some Navajo hogans about two miles ahead.

"Keep pushing!" he shouted into the rising wind. "Robert, not much farther and we'll be among Navajo!"

"But what if they hate white people!" Lucy yelled over the chasing storm.

"We've got extra horses to trade for help . . . and extra saddles," Longarm shouted back. "So they'll help us, by damned!"

There were four hogans pressed up against the red mesas, and from the cottonwoods around, Longarm figured that there must be a good spring that fed off the mesa tops down to where the Navajo families had chosen to live. They passed through a herd of goats and some sheep and small ponies. Three Navajo men armed with old black-powder pistols and what looked to be a big-bore buffalo rifle came out to confront the whites.

"We need food, medicine, and shelter from the storm," Longarm said as soon as they were close. "Do you speak English?"

The youngest of them spoke Navajo to the others and then stepped forward. "My name is Mike. I speak good English." He pointed at Robert, who was swaying in the saddle. "What is wrong with that man? Does he have smallpox? Some white man's disease that sickens and kills The People?"

"No," Longarm firmly replied. "He was beaten by bad men and is hurt. He is in need of strong medicine."

"No white man's sickness?" the Navajo asked again, looking not only suspicious but very worried.

"None. Your medicine man or woman would be able to see this if you will help."

"You have many horses. Whose horses and saddles are those that are without riders?"

"The three dead men that tortured this one owned those horses. But if you help, we will give you these two extra horses. And there is another horse back where we came, but he is old and slow."

Mike shrugged. "Maybe good eating, though."

"Yes."

"No!" Lucy cried. "That is a nice and gentle old horse."

"Mind your tongue," Longarm said harshly, knowing that if Lucy prevailed in her objection, it would make him look weak, and that was not a good thing among these people.

Lucy blanched with anger, but something in Longarm's expression made her bite her tongue in silence.

"If you help, you can have these two extra horses, and the one we left behind to eat."

The one who spoke English spoke to his companions, and there was some discussion, until Longarm felt icy raindrops and said, "We need help *now*."

The Navajo made his offer. "We take the horse you are riding and you take one of the other horses."

"No," Longarm said, shaking his head for emphasis. "I'm not giving up this buckskin mare. She is . . . she is like my woman."

The Navajo's jaw dropped, and then he threw back his head and laughed at the darkening sky. He told his companions that Longarm thought that his buckskin was like his woman, and they also burst into raucous gales of laughter.

After that, everything got friendly and Longarm knew that they would be able to weather the storm and that Robert Durham would get some good Navajo medicine.

Chapter 14

The Navajo invited them into a hogan that was many-sided
with the door facing east. Inside, a fire burned in a little
pit in the center of a room made of timbers and logs and
covered on the outside with adobe. The dimly lit interior
was cozy, and Longarm noted that there were at least eight
people seated on Navajo rugs and sheepskins. Most of
them were children, with round, dark, and curious eyes.
When the strangers entered, the women and children
moved back from the fire, where a delicious lamb stew was
simmering in an iron pot. They offered no greeting, but
watched Longarm, Lucy, and Robert with great interest.

Longarm made a quick introduction, doubting they
spoke English, yet to his surprise one of the older Navajo
girls, who wore a lovely turquoise necklace, asked, "What
happened to that poor man?"

"He was hurt very badly by other men."

"Navajo?"

"No, white men. This is his sister, Lucy. I am Custis,

and the man who is hurt is named Robert. We need help and strong Navajo medicine."

The girl, who looked to be about fifteen, spoke to several of the older women, and soon a messenger was sent to find help. Fifteen minutes later a Navajo medicine man, wearing coyote skins and with his silver hair braided and decorated with feathers, entered the hogan with an air of grave dignity. All conversation stopped, and the medicine men went to Robert's side and unbuttoned his shirt to study the extent of his injuries.

The medicine man began to chant and wave an eagle's feather at the ceiling of the hogan. The praying lasted for about five minutes, and then the old man removed several small gourds plugged with tobacco. He studied each little gourd for several minutes, speaking to it as if the gourd possessed a spirit that needed to be consulted. Satisfied, the old man went to work opening the various gourds and applying their contents to Robert. Some were liquid, some were salves, and one was a golden-colored pollen, and each was administered with a special blessing prayer. When he had finished with his ministrations, the medicine man lifted a larger gourd that had been suspended by a leather thong from around his neck, uncorked it, and then pressed it to Robert's lips.

Robert had been silent until now, but his nose twitched and he shook his head from side to side.

"He wants you to drink from the big gourd," Lucy said.

"What is it?" Robert asked weakly.

The old Navajo medicine man was not one to have either his medicine or his judgment questioned. Impatient, he tried to force the mouth of the gourd between Robert's teeth.

"No!" Robert protested, fighting and knocking the gourd away, causing it to spill some of its liquid.

"That stuff smells terrible!" Robert cried. "I can't get that down my throat."

Longarm grabbed Robert's good arm and squeezed it very hard. "Listen to me well! You'd better drink the medicine and behave, or this medicine man will feel dishonored and leave. Trust me, Robert, these people have strong medicine and you need his help."

Their eyes locked and then Robert nodded. "All right. I'll . . . I'll try to choke it down."

Robert took three large swallows and began to violently convulse and choke. The medicine man reached out and grabbed Robert's neck and throttled it as if he were dispatching a chicken bound for the stew pot. Lucy cried out and attempted to help her brother, but Longarm stopped her, saying, "He's just making sure that your brother doesn't cough any of that medicine back up."

"It could be *poison*! Even I can smell the stench of it, and I can't imagine how it must taste."

"Doesn't matter, if he helps him," Longarm told her firmly. "Lucy, maybe it would be best for you to go outside."

"It's starting to rain hard."

"Then move away and let this man do his work on your brother," Longarm ordered. "If you interfere, he will lose face and go away. Furthermore, we will have insulted these people and they will not help us. They will tell us to leave . . . storm or no storm, and we'll have no choice but to do it."

"All right, I'll get out of the way and keep my mouth shut. But . . ."

Longarm didn't let her finish. "You need to get our bedrolls off the horses right now before they're sodden. Get the rifles and anything else that needs to be kept dry and bring them inside as well."

Lucy didn't like taking orders, even from Longarm. "Anything else I can do, Your Majesty?"

"Yeah, don't be a smart aleck."

Lucy got up and stomped out of the hogan. Ten minutes later she had their blankets, provisions, and weapons stacked up against the far wall. She hurried over to her brother and then pulled back when she saw that the medicine man was setting the broken arm. Just a well-practiced and hard jerk and the arm was straight again, but Robert passed out cold.

"Nice work," Longarm said with admiration.

The younger Navajo translated the remark to the medicine man, who smiled, showing he had very few teeth. A green salve was smeared across Robert's chest and over the broken ribs and then for the next half hour prayers were offered for his swift recovery. After that, the medicine man gathered up his powerful medicines and exited the hogan, looking very dignified.

Longarm and Lucy slept side by side along with an entire Navajo family in the hogan. They could hear the storm outside and the wind whistling fiercely through trees and canyons. They heard torrents of water spilling off the mesa tops and rocks rolling down the raging river. It rained almost all night, and in the morning when they awakened, all the Navajo had left the hogan and were out gathering their scattered sheep and horses. He and Lucy watched all of the families as they spread out looking for strays.

Longarm studied the horizon and said, "It's going to

be clear today, but I'm sure that your brother is strong enough to travel."

"I spoke to him a moment after you left," Lucy said. "He's feeling better this morning."

"I knew that he would," Longarm replied. "Just as I knew he wouldn't have survived last night's storm if we'd been caught out in the open."

"Those men who tried to kill us, we left their bodies in the wash. Do you think . . ."

"They're miles away from where we left them, and probably their corpses have been torn apart by the flash flood that would have swept them off someplace.

Lucy shuddered.

"Just forget them," Longarm urged. "They made their own choices, and they gambled and lost their lives."

"The young one . . ."

"He made a choice too," Longarm interrupted. "What was done is done, and it's best to put it into the past."

"I'll try," Lucy said. "How far are we from Cortez and my ranch?"

"If I were riding hard by myself, I could probably make it in a day. But given that the dry washes are now filled with water and mud, and the fact that Robert isn't strong enough to ride, it might take us three or four days before we can get to the ranch."

"I was afraid of that," she said. "So we just have to sit tight until my brother is feeling better."

"I'm afraid so." Longarm watched as a boy no older than six was having quite a serious disagreement with a billy goat. The goat had long, curved horns and he was in a feisty mood, not wanting to be driven back to a brush pen that had been partially blown down, but already prepared for captivity.

Suddenly, a black-and-white sheepdog shot out of the brush, bit the billy on the butt, and sent it plunging toward the muddy brush corral. The boy, angry that he had been defied, picked up a rock and hurled it at the billy but missed and almost hit his dog.

"Gonna be interesting to stay among these few families for a couple of days and watch them go about their business."

"And what business might that be?" Lucy asked.

"Just stayin' alive and feeding themselves and their animals. These Navajo live in a tough country, and they don't worry too much about building up their flocks or getting rich . . . or even old. They pretty much take things day by day."

"Which I guess is what we're going to have to do."

"That's right." Longarm led Lucy out a ways from the hogans and then asked, "So do you think that there will be any more of 'em coming after you and Robert for what you took back in Philadelphia?"

Lucy took his hand and said, "You can bet on it, Custis. This isn't over yet."

"Will they keep coming?"

"I'm afraid that they will, until they either kill me or recover the money, jewelry, and precious stones that I ran off with when I came to Denver."

"Then I guess that we'll just have to go to Philadelphia as soon as we can and have a showdown."

"One that we could never win."

Longarm thought about that for a few minutes and then asked, "What would draw the old man out of Philadelphia to come here?"

"I don't know."

"Think about that real hard," Longarm urged. "Because

if there is one old man that is sending all these killers after us, then he's the one that has to either die or have a big change of heart."

"He would *never* have a change of heart."

"Then he is going to have to die if we're to have any chance of living," Longarm told her as they walked back to their hogan.

Chapter 15

Longarm and Lucy spent two more days waiting for Robert to regain his strength. They walked along the base of the towering red mesa, and sometimes, where there was a black patina on the ancient rocks, they studied the etched art of petroglyphs with great interest. Here and there they also found pictographs, small paintings mostly of animals used to tell ancient stories.

"Do you have any idea what these etchings and the paintings on the rocks say?" Lucy asked Longarm as they studied at least a half dozen of the drawings that had been left many centuries before. "For instance, that one that starts at a point in the center and goes round and round in a concentric circle?"

"I haven't a clue," Longarm admitted. "But you can see that some of these show hunters with raised spears about to kill mountain sheep and goats."

"Yes, I see that. How *old* do you think these pictographs and petroglphys might be?"

"If I had to offer a wild guess, I'd say that they are between five hundred and a thousand years old."

Lucy bent down and picked up a pottery shard and turned it this way and that admiring the simple but dramatic black-on-gray designs. "This must have come from a beautiful pot that some woman made centuries ago."

She ran her fingers gently over the broken piece of pottery and then placed it back where she'd found it. "It's comforting somehow for me to know that way back then they appreciated beauty enough to go to the trouble to decorate their clay pottery."

"Yeah," Longarm said. "And I'd give anything to know what the petroglyphs and pictographs up on these walls are trying to tell us."

"I'll bet the Navajo we are visiting know," Lucy said.

"Maybe, but even if they do, they'd never tell us the secrets their ancestors left for them to read."

Longarm sat down and his eyes roved across the hard, arid landscape. "Lucy, is the patriarch of the Horton family physically capable of getting on a train and coming out to Colorado?"

"I'm sure that he is. Philip Horton still rides on fox hunts and rules his empire with an iron hand. His oldest son, Devlin, is always at this side and is every bit as mean, ruthless, and vindictive as his father. Charles was afraid of them both and I've always thought that was why he drank so hard and lived so recklessly."

"What would it take to get the old man or his eldest son out to Colorado?" Longarm asked.

"A crisis of some sort."

Longarm frowned. "What kind of a crisis could we come up with that would do that?"

"I'm . . . I'm not sure."

"We have to find something. The idea of either Philip or Devlin sending assassin after assassin to follow you and Robert, until they eventually succeed, isn't a healthy option."

"No," Lucy agreed, "it isn't."

"Did you take anything from Philadelphia that they still might not know about? Something so valuable to their way of thinking that it would draw them here without delay?"

Lucy sat down and picked up another piece of decorated pottery. "There is something that I took that they probably don't know is missing yet and that would send them into a mindless rage."

"What is that?"

"A document," she said. "A birth certificate written by a doctor stating that Philip Horton was fathered by a common Spanish sailor from Madrid who won his mother's heart away and then was caught by the authorities and imprisoned in a dungeon until she died abandoned and long forgotten."

"So this document proves that your husband's father is a bastard," Longarm said quietly.

"That's right. Charles came upon the information by accident, and he showed the document to me one night when he was drunk. He had never known his grandmother, and his father would never even speak her name. Never allow anyone to even ask about her."

"So *this* is your father-in-law's darkest secret?"

"Yes." Lucy was silent for a few moments. "My husband was terrified of his father and that his oldest brother, Devlin, might be left with almost the entire Horton fortune. Charles believed that by secretly obtaining this document, which his father had managed to keep hidden, with its potential to disgrace his family, he had some . . . leverage if he was disinherited."

"Leverage?"

"Yes, you see, Philip Horton has long claimed that his family dates right back to the king of Sweden, that he is descended from royalty, and no one ever questioned the fact."

Longarm supposed that he understood. "So to have it revealed that his own father was nothing but a common sailor and that his mother had him out of wedlock to that man would be . . ."

"It would ruin the family name," Lucy said. "I know this is difficult for everyday people like us to understand, but in very high society, be it Boston, New York or Philadelphia, pedigree is very, very important. If the truth ever came out that Philip Horton was a bastard, he would be shunned and his standing among his peers would be destroyed."

Longarm shook his head. "That kind of thing hardly seems worth all the effort it is taking to preserve the lie."

"It is worth every bit of the effort to Philip Horton," Lucy said. "You really can't imagine the bombshell that such news would be among the rich in Philadelphia, many of whom hate Philip because he has been so ruthless in his business dealings."

"And you have this document?"

"Yes. Charles insisted that it be kept secret and hidden to be used only as a last resort."

"That being if he were disinherited."

"Exactly."

"Where is this document?"

"In a safe deposit box back in Denver. And please believe that I never thought of using it for personal gain."

"Lucy, since what you took as your rightful inheritance

is not enough to bring Philip Horton or his eldest son, Devlin, we might have to use that document to bring all of this to a showdown."

Lucy visibly shuddered and the pottery slipped from her hands. "If we did that they would all come to Denver and I can't imagine what. . . ."

Longarm put his arms around the woman. "To be very frank with you, Lucy, it seems obvious that old Philip Horton will keep sending killers until we use that document to draw him and possibly Devlin to Colorado, where I can either arrest . . . or kill them."

Lucy shuddered again, but she did not disagree.

Chapter 16

Longarm, Lucy, and Robert had thanked the Navajo people many times before they rode away from the hogans, making a straight line toward Cortez and the Canyon Ranch. For their part, the Navajo were very glad to have more horses and saddles.

Robert was still extremely weak and in considerable pain, but the medicine man had given him a few potions and salves to apply, and there was little doubt that his battered, swollen, and scabbed-over face would heal, as would his cracked ribs and broken arm.

"We were so fortunate to have stumbled across those families living under the mesa," Lucy said as they crossed into Colorado. "And you were right, Custis, Robert would have died that first night exposed to the fury of that terrible storm."

"It wasn't quite as much due to luck as you might think," Longarm confessed. "Actually, I chased an outlaw who'd robbed a bank and shot three people through this country about five years back, and although I never visited those hogans, I saw them far off in the distance."

"Did you catch the outlaw?"

"I shot him in the back with my rifle. He thought he was out of my range . . . but I'm a pretty good marksman and I used a boulder to steady my aim. I think I blew a hole in his back from about two hundred yards, and he was riding away fast."

"Quite a shot," Robert said.

"I was rather proud of it," Longarm replied.

Lucy looked troubled. "If you'd been through this country and knew of those hogans, why didn't you . . ."

"Tell you about them before the storm hit us?" Longarm guessed. "Well, you have to admit that a lot of this red-rock country, with its thousands of box canyons, pinnacles, and mesas, looks all the same. I was afraid that I might be leading us to the base of the wrong mesa and that to raise your hopes and then have to dash them, given our desperate circumstances, would have been too much to bear."

Robert, grimacing and holding on to his saddle horn, glanced at Longarm and said, "Lucy tells me that you know everything about the Horton family and their dark secrets."

"If you mean about the money, jewelry, and diamonds she took, yes."

"And also about the document that would ruin old Mr. Horton back in Philadelphia and prove that his royal ancestry is a complete fraud."

"Yes, that too," Longarm answered. "So I guess we are all finally being honest with each other and not holding anything important back?"

It was a question, and Longarm's steady gaze passed gravely from sister to brother.

"That's right," Lucy finally said. "On another subject,

do you think that anyone will be waiting at the ranch with a rifle, hoping to finish what the others could not?"

"Seems a fair possibility," Longarm answered. "Might be a good idea to ride directly into Cortez, get a room for the night, and just kind of scout things out to make sure that we don't have any more assassins waiting for you and your brother to return."

"I wouldn't mind doing that," Robert confessed. "I'd like to see a medical doctor in town."

"I understand," Longarm answered. "But I have to tell you that I doubt any medical doctor in America could have taken better care of your wounds than the old Navajo medicine man."

"I certainly agree," Lucy said. "I had never really known anything about Indians . . . just the lurid stories you hear that paint them as bloodthirsty savages . . . but after what they did for us back there, I have a whole different perspective."

"The Indian people are just as diverse as us whites. And there's as much difference between, say, a Cheyenne and a Navajo as there is between an Italian and an Englishman. It's a mistake to put people into boxes and think of them as being all the same because of their color."

"I'll remember that," Lucy said. "And if we survive the Horton family's vendetta, I'll be forever grateful and kind to the Navajo."

"The Hopi and the Ute are mighty good people as well," Longarm said, "although I've not had too much friendship with some of the other tribes that I've come across . . . especially the Apache, who have fought us right from the start, trying to hold on to their lands."

"What about the document concerning Philip Horton's true sire?"

"We'll have to go to Denver and get it," Longarm told her. "Before we start this deadly game, I want to see it with my own eyes."

"Don't you trust me?" Lucy asked, attempting to place a hurt expression on her lovely face.

"Actually, I don't," Longarm replied. "Seems like getting the truth out of you happens only when it comes from necessity. Every time we get in a bad fix, you give me a little more information."

"Custis! You've saved our lives and in the process almost lost your own several times. Why would I . . ."

"Don't ask that question," Longarm told her. "Just . . . just be straightforward and don't bullshit me anymore."

Lucy dropped the hurt expression, replacing it with one of anger. "I've no more secrets to hold from you!"

"We'll see," Longarm told her. "We'll see when we open that bank box and I have a look at that paper that I'm hoping will bring this all to a head."

"It will definitely do that," Robert promised. "But if you do what you're planning, you'd better expect that Mr. Horton, his mean-spirited son Devlin, and probably some other people just as deadly are going to come to Denver with only one purpose in mind."

"Killing all of us," Longarm said.

"That's right. And doing it slow if they can get away with it," Devlin added. "Marshal Long, you don't know what kind of people you are going to be up against."

Longarm just snorted. "I've been bushwhacked twice now. I've learned what they did to a poor woman named Lizzy, and I've seen what those three hired gunmen did to you. So there's nothing left that will surprise me about the kind of people we are going to be facing. But here is the thing, Robert. Denver is *my* town, and I've got a lot of good friends there to watch our backs. Men who are tough, brave, and smart and won't back down or away if the lead starts to flying and blood is spilling onto the ground. Understand?"

They both nodded, and Longarm prodded the buckskin mare on up ahead. He was troubled about what was going to happen next. He didn't know if there were more assassins sent from Philadelphia waiting just up ahead . . . but he'd face that very soon.

Still and all, he had a bad feeling in the pit of his stomach that neither Lucy Horton nor her beat-up and busted-up brother, Robert Durham, had told him the whole damn, sordid story. And if he had any extra money to bet, he'd bet that the surprises and killing were a long ways from being over.

Chapter 17

It was at the end of a long day's ride when they finally arrived back in Cortez. Longarm helped Robert over to the doctor's office and then turned to Lucy. "I'll look around town, but I don't think that anyone is here to kill us today."

"I'm exhausted. I'm going to get a room for Robert and myself at the hotel."

"That's fine," Longarm told her. "I'll get my own room, and we'll try to get a good night's sleep. In the morning, we can go over to the stagecoach office and get tickets for Denver."

"I sure don't want to go back," Lucy confessed.

"I understand. But going to the ranch and waiting for the next bunch of hired killers to arrive from Philadelphia doesn't make any sense. When we get to Denver, we'll find you and Robert a new place, and you can go into hiding while I wait for old man Horton or his son Devlin to show up with a few hired gunmen."

"I'm sorry this is turning out to be such a mess," Lucy told him. "You don't deserve this."

"And you didn't deserve to be treated so badly by your late husband and then have to fight for your life."

"Tell Robert that I'll be across the street at the hotel."

"I will."

Longarm relayed the message to Robert, who was being examined by the town's only doctor. "Doc says that Navajo medicine has been working real well on my injuries, Custis."

"No surprise to me," Longarm replied. "Your sister is getting a room for you and her at the hotel."

Robert frowned. "I thought you and her . . ."

"We are and we did," Longarm said quickly. "But we're all worn down and we need to get a good night's sleep. Maybe I'll see you later at the Cortez Café."

Robert nodded, and Longarm headed straight for the Gay Lady Saloon and a glass of whiskey. Molly came right over to greet him. "Glad to see you again, Custis. I saw you and Lucy Horton along with her brother ride in a while ago. Robert didn't look too good."

"He's had a rough time of it," Longarm told the saloon owner. "Three men kidnapped and then beat the hell out of him. He was half-dead by the time that his sister and I were able to overtake them some miles beyond the Four Corners."

"Is he going to be all right?"

"Your town's doctor says he will be. But we're leaving for Denver tomorrow on a stage."

"Why don't you stick around for a few days and rest up?" Molly asked, touching his sunburned and haggard face. "You look like you've ridden through hell and back."

"Can't spare the time, Molly."

"Well, can I at least buy you a drink and a dinner?"

"That you can do."

"Who knows," Molly said with a wink. "Maybe after a few drinks and with a good meal under your belt you'll feel like a man again."

"Are you suggesting something?" he asked with a grin.

"I might be. Truth is that you're pretty ripe smelling at the moment. How about you go upstairs to my place and I'll have a boy fix you up with a hot bath and a sharp razor?"

"You're setting me up for more than a meal."

"You got that right."

"First the whiskey, then the bath."

"Why not both at the same time?" Molly suggested, hand dropping between them to rub his thigh.

Longarm thought that was a fine idea. And thirty minutes later he was luxuriating in a huge, claw-footed bathtub with a bottle of good whiskey in one hand and a bar of soap in the other.

"Molly," he said, grinning and passing her the bottle. "You are an angel. I stank so bad I could smell myself, and my horse was fluttering her lips and keeping her nose up in the wind!"

Molly Martin laughed. "Water hot enough for you?"

"Sure is."

"Give me the soap and the washrag and I'll scrub your back."

"You are twice an angel."

Molly took a slug of whiskey, and then she washed his back and hair. "Feels wonderful," Longarm said with a sigh of pleasure.

"You ain't felt the half of it yet."

"What's that supposed to mean?"

"I'm sure you can guess," Molly said as she began to remove her clothing. "Stiffen up, handsome, I'm climbing in."

"No," Longarm corrected, "if you come into my bathtub you're climbing *on*."

"I was hoping that you'd be up for that," Molly said, tearing off the last of her underwear and then hopping into the tub and easing her bottom down on his stiffening manhood.

"Water is spilling over the top and all over the floor of your room."

"I'll just have someone mop it up after we're done here and gone to eat," Molly said, kissing Longarm hard. "But for now, let's just sip whiskey and do the bouncy-bouncy."

"That sounds just right," Longarm said, reaching around behind Molly and pulling her hips tight against his own. He closed his eyes and listened to the water splash on the floor and the soft moans of Molly as she worked herself into a frenzy of sexual pleasure.

It seemed impossible that only three days ago he'd been sleeping in a Navajo hogan along with about ten other people. Not that he hadn't appreciated their hospitality, but with Molly bouncy-bouncing up and down on his manhood and with good whiskey warming his shrunken belly, he felt like he had died and was now getting a preview of heaven.

Molly came first and sent waves of soapy water over the rim of the tub, and then Longarm let go and nearly lifted her completely out of the water with his own lunging climax.

"Man, that was good," Molly panted as she climbed out of the tub and then nearly slipped on the floor and fell. "Same for you?"

"Yeah," Longarm replied, standing up and reaching for the bottle. "It's been a while."

"I would have thought you and Lucy would have been doing it regularly."

"We were, in Denver."

Molly studied his sagging manhood and grinned. "After what you just gave me, I'm half-tempted to turn this place over to my manager for a week or two and come along with you."

"Not a good idea," Longarm told her. "There's going to be a showdown, and you don't want to be around when it happens."

"Want to tell me about it?"

"Okay, over a steak and a glass of good wine."

"That's a deal," Molly said. "And I've got some clean clothes that will fit you in my closet."

"What?"

"I like big men, but a few of them have been disappointing, and I threw them out of this room when they were bare-assed naked."

Longarm had a belly laugh over that one because he could just visualize Molly doing that to some man who had bragged about his abilities, only to have it come out that he was impotent or loutish in the art of lovemaking.

Molly found a fresh towel and rubbed Longarm down. When she started to dry and rub him below the belt, he gently pushed her away, saying, "I'm starved for food,

Molly. Let's eat first and then see if we're up for another round, only this time in your bed."

"I'll be ready."

"I'll probably be ready too," he said, kissing her face and then going to her closet to see just what kind of clothes he was going to have to wear to dinner.

Chapter 18

"You're coming back someday, ain't you?" Molly Martin asked, pinching Longarm on the butt as he hoisted his satchel and then himself up into the stagecoach. "I got some things that I want to show you."

"I'll just bet she does." Lucy whispered from inside the coach. "But I'd have thought that she showed you about everything she has or ever will have last night."

"Lucy," Robert said in a hushed tone of voice. "If everything goes right and we survive this ordeal, we're coming back to the ranch and we're going to want to be friends with the people in Cortez."

"I doubt that woman and I are ever going to be friends," Lucy snapped.

Longarm ignored Lucy and reached out to squeeze Molly's hand. "You take care of yourself, and I'll be back one of these days. Might do some trout fishing or . . ."

"Let's do the . . . *or* thing!" Molly giggled lewdly as the stagecoach pulled out of Cortez, heading for the high passes that would lift them over the Rockies and on to Denver.

"You both look very much rested," Longarm remarked as he settled into his seat and gazed at the pair. "Amazing what a good night's rest can do for the body."

"Too bad you forgot about that, because you look completely dragged out," Lucy snipped. "And whose clothes are you wearing?"

"Never you mind," Longarm answered, tipping his Stetson down over his eyes. "I'm going to take a nap now."

Lucy was seething, but Longarm didn't care. He had never allowed a woman to put a noose around his neck and a ring through his nose, and he'd be damned if he'd do so today.

They arrived in Denver somber and serious, knowing that this was where the showdown would end . . . one way or the other . . . with the Philadelphia Horton family. Longarm insisted that he be shown the document that Lucy said was locked in a safe deposit box, and when he did study it, he was satisfied that the paper was a legitimate birth certificate. A document that would completely destroy Philip Horton's social standing back east.

"Put it back in the box," Longarm said. "And let's go to the telegraph office."

"No waiting around."

"No," Longarm said. "And let's be very careful that there isn't someone else in Colorado sent from Philadelphia to punch our tickets."

On the way to the telegraph office, Lucy said, "You said that I needed to find a different place to live."

"It would be safest both for you and your brother."

"What about you?"

"They know where I live and how to find me," Longarm told her. "And as soon as we get you and Robert settled into a hiding place, I'll go to my office and make an official report. Like I said before, I've got plenty of support and seasoned lawmen who will watch my back until this is over."

"What if Philip Horton *doesn't* come?"

Longarm had already given that possibility considerable thought. "I've never been to Philadelphia before, but I've heard it's quite a place to visit. I'd like to see the place where the Declaration of Independence was signed by Ben Franklin and the other great founders of our nation. I'd do that, of course, before I confronted Philip and Devlin Horton."

"Excellent idea," Lucy said in a grim tone of voice as they continued on their way down the street to Denver's busy telegraph office.

Lucy had an address where the telegraph was to be delivered, and they both spent some time composing the message. In the end, it was simple and read:

Mr. Philip Horton

Have proof of your real parentage. Will release information to every newspaper between Denver and Philadelphia unless paid $10,000 cash. Contact me at the Porter House in person within two weeks . . . or else. Come alone.

The telegraph operator scratched his head. "This message is . . . unusual. No name attached to the telegram?"

"Not necessary."

The operator looked troubled. "We do have strict rules about the contents that we send, and this message seems like . . ."

"It's official business."

Longarm produced his United States marshal's badge, and the operator nodded with sudden understanding. "Of course, Marshal. The charge for sending the message and having a runner deliver it to this Philadelphia address will be eight dollars and thirty-three cents."

"I'll pay that," Lucy said, opening her purse.

When the message had been sent, Longarm escorted Lucy back onto the street. "You will, of course, *not* be staying at the Porter House. At least not under your own name"

"Then what . . ."

"I'll register a room under your name and I'll stay there and wait. No hurry, really, unless Philip has a few more killers waiting here in Denver."

"He might," Lucy said. "The man has more money than he can possibly spend, and when he gets that message, he'll go berserk."

"We need to draw him here," Longarm told her. "We have to cut the head off the snake."

"Where are you staying tonight?" Lucy asked.

"I was thinking about staying in my own room."

"Would you like some companionship?"

"Is that a proposition, Lucy?"

"I guess that it is, although I'm quite disappointed with you spending the last night in Cortez with that saloon woman."

"Molly Martin owns that saloon, and she's a fine woman despite what you might think of her," Longarm said defensively. "And if that's how you're going to act, then this is where we part ways."

"Wait!" Lucy sighed. "I'm sorry. And you're right. I have no right to judge anyone."

"Then we'll hear no more of that talk," Longarm said, eyeing her closely. "And I need that as your promise."

"I promise."

Longarm was satisfied. "We'll have a nice dinner after we go up to my room. These clothes really are too tight and uncomfortable."

"You look ridiculous with the pants up around your ankles," Lucy told him.

"Then I'll take them off the minute we go through my door . . . but you have to take advantage of that fact."

"It's a deal," Lucy said, squeezing his hand.

Longarm paraded down the street, aware that other young men were staring at Lucy, who was so attractive that it was nearly impossible to keep your eyes off her, and to not drool with lust when they were on her.

"It's a good day," he said. "Might be fun to go have a picnic along Cherry Creek as soon as possible."

"I don't think so," she said. "Because that's where all this trouble began."

"No, it didn't. It began when you married into the Horton family and then learned that your husband was a wastrel, a drunk, and a first-rate asshole."

"Yeah, it did," Lucy said. "It really did."

Chapter 19

Later that day Longarm helped Lucy and her brother get registered in separate rooms, under assumed names, at the Porter House and then he hurried over to his office to see his boss, Marshal Billy Vail.

"Well!" Billy said, rising up from his office chair and smiling. "So you're finally back."

"Yeah, I'm back."

"You've lost a lot of weight and look pretty ragged," Billy said, smile dying. "What happened over at Cortez?"

Longarm recounted the whole story, with Billy sitting on the edge of his seat. When he was finished, Billy leaned back and laced his stubby fingers behind his head.

"Custis, you've had quite a time with this Philadelphia woman. I hope that she stays in Cortez and this whole bloody episode is over."

"I'm afraid that it isn't, Billy. Mrs. Horton and her brother returned to Denver with me. I just helped them get registered at the Porter House. Furthermore, I've sent an explosive telegram to a Mr. Philip Horton in Philadelphia. He's the one that has been sending men out here to kill Lucy and her brother."

"The reason being?"

Longarm told his boss about the social devastation that would befall the rich old man if his true ancestry became known. He ended up saying, "I know this doesn't seem like a huge thing to us, Billy, but apparently it would ruin Philip Horton and his powerful Eastern family."

"That may be true, but it's hardly a sufficient reason for sending killers our way."

"I agree."

"And you don't think that the real reason for all this bloodshed is because Mrs. Horton and her brother stole a lot of the old man's jewelry, cash, and diamonds?"

"She didn't steal anything that didn't belong to her. She was cheated and disinherited. However, I'm sure that's a big part of it as well."

"Undoubtedly. And remember this, there are usually two sides to every story. What if the woman actually stole a fortune that didn't belong to her?"

"Not possible," Longarm said. "She is telling the truth."

"So she says and so you say."

"I'd stake my reputation on it, Billy."

"All right," the man said, conceding the point. "But still and all it seems that Philip Horton has gone way past a simple desire for revenge."

"He has and I'll tell you why. But first, let me ask you this. Billy, have you ever known anyone that was *really* rich and powerful with a long and distinguished family background?"

"Can't say that I have. I've known a few wealthy men,

but most of them were self-made . . . you know, prospectors who hit it big. Maybe a few businessmen here in Denver who were in the right place at the right time and worked their butts off and became well-to do. But *old school* wealth . . . nah. I haven't known anyone in that class."

"I did when I was growing up in West Virginia. Plantation owners, mostly. Some were slave traders, others made fortunes on the high seas and built shipping fleets. I never actually knew these families well, but I was around them, and I observed enough to know that with these people respect for their family name means everything. So it's not hard for me to imagine that a very wealthy and well-connected family from Philadelphia would go to any length to preserve their good name and reputation."

"And having a bastard at the helm that had been fathered by a lowly sailor would destroy all that."

"It would," Longarm said emphatically. "So mark my words, the old man or his son Devlin *will* come to Denver when they receive our telegraph asking for extortion money and demanding a firm deadline."

"What telegram are you talking about?"

"I guess I forgot to mention that part of it."

"You sure as hell did. What did you send and why?"

Longarm recited the short telegram despite Billy's groans of disbelief. When he was finished, Billy said, "Well, Custis, you've really done it this time."

"I could see no other way to put an end to this vendetta."

Billy climbed out of his chair and paced back and forth for a few moments. "You're going to need help and protection."

"So are Lucy and Robert."

"I don't have an unlimited budget here, Custis. And this kind of thing really falls under the jurisdiction of the local authorities."

"You know they won't lift a finger. Sheriff Goddard answers to the citizens and voters of Denver, and he'll turn a deaf ear on all this trouble."

"I'm sure that's true," Billy had to agree. "And even worse, if Goddard learns what you've done that might create a bloodbath on his streets, he's going to be madder than hell. He might even arrest Mrs. Horton and her brother on some trumped up charge."

"That's why we have to keep Sheriff Goddard and his office out of it entirely."

"I agree," Billy said, shaking his head. He stopped his pacing and said, "Any idea when this rich old bastard and his son might arrive in Denver?"

"It will be within two weeks."

"And we don't even know what he and his son look like."

"Lucy does. She can give our people good descriptions. Better yet, she can meet each arriving train from the East and watch for them."

"All right," Billy said, "let's suppose we do spot them getting off the train here in Denver. I really don't see what we can do about it since they will not have committed a *provable* crime."

"Good god, Billy! I've killed almost a half dozen of those Philadelphia assassins! What . . ."

"But can we *prove* that they were sent by Mr. Philip Horton or his son Devlin? Do you have that proof for a judge?"

"No," Longarm grudgingly admitted. "I do not."

"Be nice if you'd just wounded one of them and he confessed that he'd been hired by the Philadelphia Horton family to come out and murder Lucy and her brother. But then that isn't the way you operate, is it?"

"When I'm shot at, I shoot back to kill," Longarm said stubbornly. "I don't see that as a fault in a lawman."

"Actually, neither do I."

Billy plunked back down in his chair. "All right, Custis. I'll pick a few men and we'll start watching the train station. You and Lucy, of course, will have to be there as well."

"Goes without speaking."

Billy made a face. "Do you have any idea of the value of what Mrs. Lucy Horton took from that Eastern estate?"

"A lot. Enough to buy a nice ranch and eventually stock it with cattle. Enough to make her and her brother well off by any standard."

"If they survive to enjoy that wealth."

"I mean to see that they do, Billy."

"Are you after her money?"

Longarm barked a cold laugh. "You know me better than that!"

"Yeah, sorry I even asked. I know what you're after, and it isn't worth all the blood that has been shed and is yet to be shed."

"You haven't seen her naked, Billy. And you haven't mounted her, so you don't know what you're talking about."

"Get out of here!" Billy howled with mock anger. "You've just *disgusted* me."

"I just told you the truth, Boss. See you later."

"Where are you going now?"

"Think I'll go to the Porter House and tuck Lucy into bed and maybe do the same for myself."

"You should be fired!"

"Thanks for your understanding," Longarm said with a wave and a chuckle as he passed out the office door.

Chapter 20

Longarm and Lucy Horton kept mostly out of sight for the next few days. Sometimes, Longarm would have Lucy walk down the street while he stood at some distance watching to see if she was being followed by another Philadelphia killer.

She never was.

However, near the end of the first week they began to start closely watching each incoming train and studying each person who arrived in Denver.

"No," Lucy would say whenever an older man would disembark. "That's not Philip."

"Are you sure? It's very likely that he'll arrive wearing a disguise."

"Philip Horton stands well over six feet tall, and he has a long, deeply lined face. His son, Devlin, is even taller and very thin, with black hair. There isn't any way they are going to be able to disguise themselves."

Longarm was growing impatient and just wanted to have this showdown over. "I hope one or both come."

"They will," Lucy promised. "That telegram will force them to come here with ten thousand dollars, which they will have no intention of giving to me."

"I'm sure the only thing they want to give you or your brother is an early grave."

Lucy dipped her chin in agreement.

"All right," Longarm said after another ten minutes of waiting. "I think everyone has gotten off the train. We might as well . . ."

His next words were forgotten as he saw a tall young man cautiously peer out of the dining coach window. It was a handsome face, but one that revealed a grim purpose. "Lucy?"

She had turned to leave and go back to her hotel, but the tone of his voice made Lucy whirl around and stare.

"That's Devlin Horton!" she whispered, ducking behind the corner of a storage shed. "That's him!"

Longarm hastily back-pedaled to join her. "Are you absolutely sure?"

"Of course I am. What are we going to do now?"

"We wait and watch," Longarm interrupted. "We need to see if Devlin's father has also come to Denver."

For ten minutes, while all the arriving passengers were greeted and then dispersed, Longarm and Lucy studied the dining car and every possible exit from the train. They saw nothing more of Devlin or his father.

"Why doesn't he just get off!" Lucy groaned with rising exasperation. "I'm going crazy!"

"Maybe Devlin and whoever he came with did get off but on the other side of the train, where they couldn't be seen."

"What do we do now?"

Longarm thought fast. "You stay here and watch, but don't allow yourself to be seen by anyone on the train. I'll walk up the tracks and then jump over the coupling and search for them up on the other side of the train."

Lucy shook her head in a panic-stricken daze. "I don't even remember what's on the other side."

"Dingy saloons, gambling parlors, and whorehouses. Plenty of places for anyone to disappear and hide."

Lucy looked skeptical. "Philip Horton is a monster, but he's a spoiled monster, and neither he nor Devlin would go into places that low."

"They would if they thought they'd otherwise be stepping into a trap that we'd set for them," Longarm told her. "Stay here. Don't move, don't do anything, until I return."

Longarm took off running, trying to keep buildings and storage sheds between him and the view of anyone watching from inside the train. He ran six cars up and then hopped over the coupling while drawing his gun. His head swiveled rapidly in both directions, for he was almost sure that he would see two tall men moving away from the train yard into one of the shanties or saloons on the wrong side of Denver's tracks.

But he saw nothing.

Longarm waited ten anxious minutes, and when no one appeared, he decided to board the train and search it car by car. If the Horton men were still hiding in the dining car or some other car, then he'd have to make a quick decision as to what to say or do.

"Hey!" a conductor yelled as Longarm burst into a coach. "What are you doing in here?"

"Forgot my luggage."

"I've never seen you before. You weren't on the train coming down from Cheyenne!"

"Forgot to buy a ticket," he said, dashing past the confused conductor and moving through the cars with his gun now half-hidden in the pocket of his coat, ready to be fired in an instant.

He could still hear the conductor yelling at him as he passed through the train, but Longarm was moving fast now. He glanced into each sleeping compartment, and when he came to the dining car where they'd seen Devlin peering through the window, he paused.

"Here goes," he said to himself, then cocked back the hammer of his Colt and burst into the car.

It was empty.

Longarm barged through the dining car, then four more cars to the back, before he reached the caboose.

Nothing!

He spun on his heels, ran to the end of the caboose, and threw himself out the back door. He leaned on the railing then jumped down and ran as hard as he could toward where he'd left Lucy.

She was gone!

Chapter 21

Longarm couldn't believe she was missing! Had Lucy been caught by surprise and overpowered? It could even have been accomplished by one of Philip Horton's assassins who had come earlier and had just been biding his time waiting for the chance to grab her and force her to give up her father-in-law's birth certificate and the wealth she had taken when she'd fled Philadelphia.

Or had she . . . and it killed him to even consider the idea . . . lied and tricked him from the beginning and gone voluntarily with someone, leaving him to look like a fool and worse?

"Damnation!" Longarm swore, knowing that she could not have gone far in the short time he'd been searching through the train. "I have to find her!"

Longarm had no idea where to begin looking for the missing woman. He felt a terrible urgency, in case she really had been kidnapped and would be tortured until she handed over that birth certificate and all the wealth she'd brought from the East.

"Hey!" a man shouted.

Longarm whirled, gun in hand, to see Hank Allen, one of the federal marshals assigned to his office and to protect Lucy. "What the hell is going on!"

"Lucy Horton is missing. I left her here while I searched the train and told her not to move."

Allen was a good man, fairly new to the job, but Longarm had judged him to be smart, brave, and honest. "Hank, you go in that direction and I'll go this way. If you overtake Lucy, she might be with two men, one old and one about your age. The men are both tall, and I'm sure they are armed and dangerous."

"Shall I arrest them?"

Longarm wanted to tell this young federal marshal that he should arrest all of them . . . even Lucy . . . but something told him that would be more than the inexperienced deputy United States marshal could safely handle.

"No," he decided, "just follow them to wherever they go. Don't allow yourself to be spotted, and when they come to rest, find me if I haven't already found you."

"All right," Marshal Allen said, taking off at a run.

Longarm hurried away in the opposite direction, hoping it was he who overtook Lucy and the Horton men. Hoping that they didn't kill her and hoping that she hadn't lied to him from the very start.

He was rushing up West Colfax Avenue near the gold-domed Colorado State Capitol Building when he finally caught a glimpse of Lucy and her captors cutting across the grassy and heavily treed capitol grounds.

Turning sharply in their direction, Longarm sprinted

after the trio, and as he began to close the ground, he saw that Lucy was stumbling and that the man he assumed to be Devlin Horton had a rope or perhaps a sash cord around her neck and was yanking her onward. The heavier man at his side was hobbling, trying to keep up with his two younger companions.

Longarm knocked over a vendor selling peanuts and heard his angry shouts. As he drew closer, he pulled his gun and then bellowed, "Stop or I'll shoot!"

Both men turned with guns in their hands. Longarm saw the older man take aim, while his son placed the muzzle of his six-gun against the side of Lucy's head.

"I'll kill her!" Devlin Horton screamed. "Marshal, drop your gun or I'll kill her *now*!"

Longarm skidded to a stop. The older man fired, and Longarm felt a bullet pluck his jacket, tearing away a pocket. He returned fire twice, and the old man doubled up, bellowing with more rage than pain, gun coughing bullets into the lush lawn.

Everyone and everything froze as Philip Horton crashed to the grass, twitching, gasping, coughing up blood, and screaming his dying curses.

"Drop the gun or I'll blow her brains out!" Devlin ordered, cocking back the hammer of his pistol.

"Shoot him!" Lucy yelled. "Shoot him or we're *both* going to die!"

Longarm swallowed hard, knowing she was probably right. He dropped his gun and started to raise his hands overhead. Devlin grinned and shot him in the upper leg before he jerked Lucy up on her toes, choking and gasping. Longarm rolled behind a tree, half-expecting the man to drag Lucy over and then to execute them both on the spot.

Instead, Devlin Horton dragged Lucy away, and Long-arm's last vision of her showed that her face was no longer beautiful, but purplish and contorted with suffering and anguish. She disappeared around a building, and when Longarm tried to climb to his feet, gather his pistol, and pursue the pair, he collapsed.

Longarm grabbed his thigh, trying to staunch the flow of blood that spurted between his fingers. Had the bullet pierced an artery? he wondered for a moment, and then he didn't remember a thing.

Chapter 22

Longarm was released from the hospital four days later. Against his objections, he was secretly moved to a supply room in the Federal Building where a cot was placed and where he would be looked after and safeguarded until he was able to resume his duties.

"I'm sorry I didn't get to you sooner," Deputy Marshal Hank Allen apologized. "After leaving the passenger platform at the train station, I doubled back around the block and heard the gunshots coming from the capitol grounds. By the time I got to you, it was almost too late. You were losing so much blood, I thought sure that you were going to die. You would have, if a doctor hadn't been on the grounds and able to get that vein in your thigh clamped off."

"I was lucky as hell," Longarm said weakly. He gave the younger man a wink. "And it wasn't at all your fault, Hank. Though I'm not ashamed to say that I wish it was you that had been shot instead of me."

It was a poor effort at making a joke but very much appreciated by the younger deputy. "We'll get her back."

"Oh, I'm sure we will in time," Longarm replied. "I just hope that when we do, she's not in small pieces."

Hank Allen nodded with understanding. "At least that old bastard is dead. You gave him two bullets to the guts. It took him almost an hour to die, and there wasn't a minute of it that he wasn't cursing like a sailor."

"Like his real father might have done," Longarm said.

"Yeah."

"Tell our boss that I need to talk to him."

"He's had one hell of a time keeping Sheriff Goddard from coming in here and reaming your ass," Allen explained. "The local authorities are ready to string you up for putting everyday citizens and even some state assemblymen and senators in real danger during that capitol grounds shoot-out."

"Couldn't be helped," Longarm said. "Besides, that's water under the bridge."

When Marshal Billy Vail arrived, Longarm asked him to close the closet door and take a seat.

"How are you feeling, Custis?"

"Never better," he deadpanned.

"You nearly bled to death on the state capitol lawn."

"So I've been told. Any news on Lucy?"

"No. I've had our men out scouring the city. They've been watching all the hotels, the train station again, stagecoach offices and liveries. Anyplace at all that this Devlin could have taken Mrs. Horton. We've got Robert Durham hidden where he can't be found."

"Lucy is probably being held hostage on the other side

of the tracks, in the criminal part of town. Devlin will have enough money to bribe anyone. He might have hired men to surround and protect him. What is driving me crazy is wondering if Lucy is still alive."

"I've been thinking a lot about that," Billy admitted. "Here's the thing. That birth certificate in Lucy's bank deposit box is our bait. It's our bait because, even though it proves only that the late Philip Horton was indeed illegitimate and a bastard, it still puts a big stain on the family, even with him gone. And that is something that I believe the eldest son will be determined to eliminate. I don't think this is mainly about the diamonds and other things that Lucy took when she ran away from Philadelphia."

"What if Devlin just decides to torture Lucy into telling him where the diamonds and money she took are hidden, then kills her and goes back to Philadelphia?"

"He could do that, but I took the liberty of placing a daily ad in the Denver paper stating that if any harm comes to the woman, we'll get a court order to open the deposit box and make the document public . . . especially to the newspapers in Philadelphia."

"Good thinking."

"Glad you approve."

"But how could Devlin get it out of the bank without Lucy's help?"

"He can't. We've already instructed the head of that bank to warn and alert every one of his employees that Devlin Horton . . . probably under disguise and an assumed name . . . will attempt to get to that deposit box."

"He'd have to have Lucy with him."

"That's right, and anyone who works at the bank will

remember her, if for no other reason than she is strikingly beautiful."

"Then we wait until he makes his move for the bank."

"We're not going to wait . . . We'll keep on searching for him and Mrs. Horton. In the meantime, I'm having plenty of good, wholesome food delivered here for you, three times a day. The doctor says you have to eat big meals and drink a lot of milk and water to replenish the blood you lost."

"Whiskey and beer will build me up faster," Longarm told his boss. "Always has, always will."

"No dice. I expect you to be back on duty in one week . . . or less."

"You can count on that," Longarm told his boss. "As soon as I'm strong enough, I'm going after Devlin and any other sons of bitches he might have brought with him from Philadelphia or hired since the shoot-out."

"We'll talk about that in a few days," Billy said.

"Sure, we can talk about it, but if you think I'm going to hide in this cramped little cubbyhole while Lucy is hostage to Devlin Horton, you've got another think coming."

"Don't try my patience any more than you already have, Custis. I've had a boatful of horseshit from Sheriff Goddard, and you might just have ruined the relationship between our departments for years."

"I only did what had to be done," Longarm insisted. "My failure was allowing Devlin to take Lucy off someplace and do god only knows what to her in the meantime."

"I'll order you a steak dinner tonight with lots of potatoes, vegetables, soup, bread . . . the works. In the meantime, get some rest."

"I could do with a good bottle of red wine with the steak, Billy."

"Sure, and I could do with the tooth fairy leaving me a thousand dollars under my pillow tonight," he replied as he left the cramped little supply room.

Chapter 23

Three days later, Billy rushed into the supply room, where Longarm was napping. "We think we've spotted Devlin Horton!"

"Where?"

He was wearing a wig, but because he is really tall and thin, one of our deputies figured he might be our man and trailed him from downtown to the other side of town."

Longarm sat up and reached for his boots, hat, and gunbelt. "Exactly where on the other side of town?"

"Are you sure you're ready for this?" Billy asked.

"I've never been more ready for anything. Where, dammit?"

"There is an abandoned brick building on the other side of Cherry Creek. It used to be a brewery, but it went out of business about six years ago. It was called Mountain Beer Brewery."

"I know the place. Did our man actually see Devlin enter that old building?"

"Yes."

"And did he wait to see if the man came back out?"

"No, he came straight here, and I've come straightaway to you."

"Any other people coming or going from that building?"

"We don't know."

Longarm reached for his coat. He buckled his gunbelt around his waist and was surprised to see that it cinched up a lot more than it had in times past. He really was off about twenty pounds.

"I have a livery outside that will take us to the vicinity. That way, you won't use up all your strength hiking across town."

"All right. Let's move."

Longarm was feeling light-headed when he climbed into the livery wagon, and he took deep breaths as it bumped along the cobblestone streets and then over the railroad tracks to a more disreputable part of town. A part of Denver where the prostitutes and cardsharps, pimps and drunks lived, fought, cheated, and schemed.

"This is close enough," Billy said. "I've already got men hidden around the building. If Devlin is in there with Mrs. Horton, he isn't going to get away from us this time."

"That's fine," Longarm gritted. "But the main thing is that we save Lucy if she is still alive."

"I'm pretty sure that she will be."

Longarm climbed out of the livery wagon and checked his gun. He followed Billy to a vantage point behind a high, wooden fence, where they met Hank Allen.

"See anyone coming or going?" Billy asked his other deputy marshal.

"Yeah. Three men in suits. They entered the building carrying some sacks and boxes."

"Probably food and drink," Longarm said. "They look like gunmen or Easterners?"

Allen nodded. "They looked . . . different. Like they didn't belong in this part of town."

Longarm pulled his pocket watch from his vest and studied it. "It's going to be dark soon. We'll wait until then and go in after Lucy."

"Now, hold on," Billy protested. "I'm the one who is in charge here and I'll make the decisions."

"All right," Longarm said. "Tell me *your* plan."

"I don't have one . . . quite yet."

"That's what I thought," Longarm said, looking straight into the man's eyes. "And by the time you put *your* plan in motion, Sheriff Goddard and his people will have caught wind of what we're up to and we'll have lawmen crawling all over this area. Devlin has hired gunmen and he's no fool. He'll post a lookout on the second or third floor. When he sees all the local and federal lawmen surrounding that old brewery, he'll turn desperate, and that's when he'll probably kill Lucy."

Billy shook his head back and forth. "That's all guesswork, Custis."

"Is it?" Longarm asked. "Obviously, I never knew Philip or his son Devlin, but Lucy told me about them and from what I gathered, they are wild and willing to do anything. Furthermore, they're all hard drinkers. So do you think that if Devlin has Lucy in that building and he's sucking up whiskey, he's really going to be reasonable?"

Billy looked away.

"I'm going to sneak in there as soon as it gets dark."

"Not without me," Billy said.

"You've been out of action for several years, Billy. No offense, but you've slowed down a lot, and I'd rather do this alone."

"I'll go in with him, sir."

They both turned to Hank Allen. Longarm spoke first. "Have you ever killed a man, Hank?"

"No."

"Can you kill a man?"

"I can," the young deputy promised. "And I'm the best shot in the whole department . . . except you, of course. Please. I met Mrs. Horton. She was kind to me, even if she is rich and a runaway. I'd like to do this. It's the reason why I wear my badge."

Longarm looked to Billy, and he could read that his boss was going to say no and choose a more seasoned lawman, but Longarm cut him off first by saying, "I'd like Hank to go in with me."

"Why him?" Billy asked.

"Just a gut feeling that he's going to be the man to help me save Lucy if she's still alive, and take care of whatever else needs taking care of in that building."

"Maybe I should send in five or six," Billy mused, clearly troubled.

"It'll be dark, and even if they have lamps or candles in there, it will be hard to spot the targets and get to Lucy. Too many men will guarantee that this will be a botch-up."

"Okay," Billy agreed. "But on one condition."

"Let's hear it."

"I go in as the third man, with a shotgun."

Longarm didn't like that, but he knew by the set of Billy's jaw that he'd gotten as many concessions as he was going to get and that he'd better not argue any longer.

"Fair enough, Boss. Get a shotgun to us, because as

soon as the sun goes down, we are going into that brewery, and their blood is going to flow like beer."

"Hank?"

"Yes, sir!"

"Go find me a double-barreled shotgun and some extra ammunition. Bring a candle and some matches as well. And Marshal Allen?"

"Yes, sir?"

"If you're not back in half an hour, we're going in without you."

"I'll be back, sir. You can count on it."

"Then go!"

When the young lawman was gone, Billy turned to Longarm and said, "I hope to God you are right about this and we're not charging into a death trap."

"If you change your mind about going in, Billy, I'll understand. You've got a pretty little wife and some kids. A fine house and a well-paying job. You don't need to go with me and Hank."

"Yes I do," Billy countered. "I may be a little fat and a little slow, but I'm still a lawman to the core, and I can carry my own weight in a bad situation. I won't get either of you killed, and I will do my part."

Longarm clapped his boss on the shoulder. "I never doubted that for a moment, Billy. Not for a single moment."

The two friends stood toe-to-toe and peered into each other's eyes, and then both of them smiled as they waited for Deputy Hank Allen and the shotgun.

Chapter 24

"Let's go!" Longarm said.

"My men are ready if anyone gets past us and tries to escape," Billy said. "No one is going to leave that brewery alive without surrendering."

Longarm was only partly listening as he moved with a pronounced limp across the weed-choked expanse between the tracks and the old brewery. He couldn't see even the smallest light inside the abandoned building, but he knew that somewhere inside Devlin and his men . . . and hopefully Lucy . . . would be hiding.

"Lucky Lucy," Longarm whispered as he made his way silently to the heavy front door of the brewery, "be lucky tonight!"

The door wasn't locked, and that wasn't surprising, given that most of the lower-floor windows had long since been broken by rock-throwing hoodlums or just angry and hopeless drunkards. Longarm was sure that some drunks and opium users probably had slept in the old building, but had recently been chased out by Devlin and his henchmen.

Longarm went inside the brewery building first, gun in hand. Hank Allen was close on his heels, and the young deputy was so tense Longarm thought he could hear the man's heart pounding over their faint footsteps.

Longarm struck a match to the candle that Hank Allen had given him only a few minutes earlier. It was a risk to light the candle, but he shielded most of its light with the palm of his hand and allowed just enough so that that he could survey the interior of the cavernous building.

What Longarm saw was hundreds of old oak beer barrels, most overturned, some burned as firewood by derelicts in the desperate grip of a freezing winter. He saw empty tins of long-used-up food and lots and lots of empty whiskey bottles . . . most shattered. Longarm saw matches and smelled urine and human shit.

This building was a nightmare, but the worst of the nightmare was still to unfold.

He motioned Hank and Billy to follow him and to be careful not to step on broken glass or empty tins or to trip over debris. They moved forward slowly across the big brewing floor, and then Longarm saw a thin blade of light under a closed door.

"There they are," he whispered.

Billy eased both hammers back on the shotgun, and Longarm paused a moment to learn if that distinctly ominous sound had penetrated the closed door. After a minute, he decided that it had not.

"We're going to bust into that room, and the first thing we need to do is to make sure that we don't accidentally kill Lucy," he hissed. "Ready?"

Both men silently nodded.

Even with a bad leg, Longarm moved with the sure stealth and speed of a catamount. He left Hank and Billy in his wake, and when he reached the door, he threw it open with his gun up and ready.

It happened so very, very fast. Five men all drinking around a table and chairs illuminated by a kerosene lamp. Food was spread across the table, which was covered with fresh white linen. A woman sat huddled alone in the far, dim corner of the room, head resting on her chest.

"Hey!" one of the men shouted.

Longarm opened fire. He was dimly aware as he pulled the trigger of his Colt revolver that bodies were jerking and men were shrieking and trying to pull out their own guns.

Devlin tried to reach Lucy and use her as his shield and only possible salvation. Billy Vail blew the tall man's head clean off his shoulders while he was in mid-stride. The head exploded against the wall, blood showering the room.

More thunder of gunfire and death wails and then . . . then absolute silence.

Not a single moan. Not a single body twitching. Only Lucy staring at Longarm with her face sheeted in blood.

It was over.

Longarm limped over to her, feeling the soles of his boots slipping on fast-pooling blood. The white tablecloth was soaked and covered with bone, brain, gristle, and gore.

"Lucy," he said, kneeling down in front of her. "We need to get out of here right now."

She was in shock and just stared at him.

"Lucy, it's Custis, and you're never going to have to worry about the Horton family again. It's *finally* going to be all right."

A single word formed on her lips. "Robert?"

"He's safe. You're both safe now."

A light . . . perhaps a ray of hope burst into her eyes, and she threw her arms around him. "I love you, Custis. I'll always love you for this."

"I know. But it wasn't just me, it was them too."

She looked over his shoulder at the pudgy, middle-aged marshal with the shotgun clenched in his fists, both barrels still smoking. Then she turned her gaze for a moment on the young man, his face pale but his jaw set with pride and purpose.

"I love you all!" she choked out as Longarm helped her to stand.

"Lucy," he whispered into her ear, "you're going to be happy in Cortez, and one day you won't even be able to remember all this blood, death, and horror."

Lucy nodded, and then she threw her arms around Longarm's neck, kissing him and crying with happiness.

Watch for

LONGARM AND NAUGHTY NELLIE

the 404th novel in the exciting LONGARM
series from Jove

Coming in July!

GIANT-SIZED ADVENTURE FROM AVENGING ANGEL LONGARM.

BY TABOR EVANS

penguin.com/actionwesterns

M456AS0510

DON'T MISS A YEAR OF

Slocum Giant
by
Jake Logan

penguin.com/actionwesterns

M457AS0510

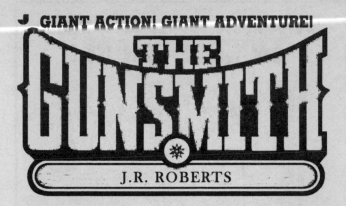

GIANT ACTION! GIANT ADVENTURE!

THE GUNSMITH

J.R. ROBERTS

penguin.com/actionwesterns

M455AS0510

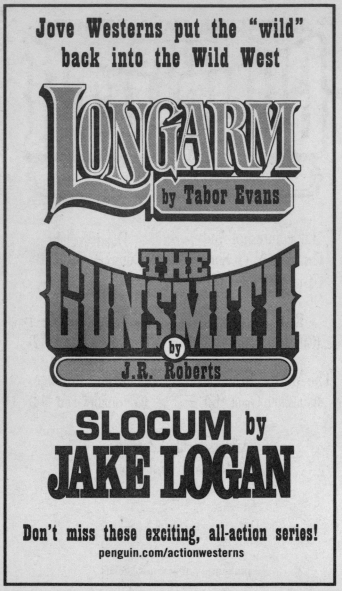